Grimm's Furry Tail

by

Kathi Daley

Chapter 1

Sunday June 7

There are moments in your life you remember with a clarity that is so vivid it seems burned into your memory. Those moments are usually the big ones that define who you are and who you will become. But there are also small moments, incidents that seem inconsequential at the time but end up serving as the catalyst that changes everything you thought you knew to be true.

For me one such moment occurred in the middle of the night when I was awakened by a dripping faucet. I tried to ignore the steady rhythm of the plop, plop-plop, plop, plop-plop, but the longer I tried to ignore the invasive noise, the more it seemed to beckon me. I swear, the steady one-two beat of the water hitting a solid surface seemed to chant the word *Em-ily*, *Em-ily*, over and over again.

I uncurled myself from the tangled mass of limbs attached to the bed hog I sleep with—my dog Max—and pulled back the covers. On the surface it might not seem that a steady drip would become one of the big moments in my life, but if not for that dripping faucet, I would never have gone downstairs, and if I hadn't gone downstairs I would never have heard the scratching at the door. And if I hadn't heard the scratching on the door, I would never have met Emily, and that, it turns out, would have made all the difference.

"What are you doing out here all by yourself?" I bent down and picked up the small orange kitten. She was a longhair cutie with a round face and curious eyes that seemed to look directly into mine. I scratched the kitten under the chin and she immediately began to purr as I cuddled her to my chest.

"Let me guess. Your name is Emily. I suppose Tansy sent you?" Tansy is one of two intuits —some say witches—who live in nearby Pelican Bay. I'm not sure why the ritual was initiated in the first place, but it seems that when I have a mystery to solve, Tansy sends a feline friend with the clues I'll need.

"I bet you're cold. And hungry. Are you hungry?" I asked the kitten.

The kitten climbed from my arms onto my chest and nestled her head under my long hair. I looked at the clock and realized it was 4:30 a.m. A bit early to get up, but by the time I saw to Emily, it was probably going to be too late to go back to bed.

I tossed another log on the smoldering fire and turned on the coffeepot. I located a can of kitten food in the pantry, then set its contents on the kitchen floor with fresh water. Emily attacked the food as if she hadn't eaten in a week. I had to wonder where the tiny kitten had come from. We have a lot of feral cats on Madrona Island, which is why Aunt Maggie founded the Harthaven Cat Sanctuary, which is housed on the oceanfront property where Maggie and I live. Emily seemed too friendly to be a feral kitten, but much too young to be out on her own if she'd been born into a domestic situation.

Once Emily was busy with her meal I scurried upstairs to find a sweatshirt to put on over my pj's. Max looked up from his place underneath my covers and watched as I rummaged through my dresser for my thick wool socks. In spite of the fact that it was June, the fog had rolled in during the night and there was a dampness in the air that made it seem colder than it actually was.

I looked out my bedroom window toward the sea that was little more than twenty-five yards from my back deck. Although I could hear the sound of the gently lapping waves, the thick mist veiled my view of the water. Of course, the sun had yet to rise, so it was still dark, but on a clear night when the moon reflected off the water, it created a magnificent picture that was truly hard to duplicate.

Max reluctantly climbed from the bed and followed me downstairs when he realized I'd decided to get up. I let him out the side door before I headed into the kitchen to check on our tiny guest. I frowned as I poured my first cup of coffee for the day. The steady drip that had awakened me in the first place could no longer be heard. I checked the kitchen sink, as well as the sink in the bathroom and the shower. In spite of the dripping I swear I'd heard, all the faucets appeared to be dry.

I returned to the kitchen and picked up the small feline. I held her so we were staring into each other's eyes. "So now that you're here, what am I to do with you? Don't get me wrong; it's not that I don't appreciate your stopping by, it's just that I only just solved a murder yesterday, my second in as many weeks, and I'm not sure I'm up for another adventure quite so soon. Any chance you made your way to the wrong porch?"

The kitten swatted at my nose. It seemed obvious that she, at least, believed she was at the correct house. Even if Tansy had sent her, I couldn't imagine that this tiny thing, who couldn't weigh more than a couple of pounds, could help me with whatever mystery she was here to help me solve.

Max barked at the door as I pondered the situation. I tucked the kitten against my chest and walked across the room. I opened the front door and Max trotted in. He lay down flat on the living room floor. I set Emily in front of the patient dog and let her approach. One of the most awesome things about my very special dog is that he seems to have a knack for making friends with the feline visitors who share our life.

"Max this is Emily; Emily, Max," I introduced.

The kitten walked over to Max and pawed him in the face. Max licked the kitten, who then pounced on Max's head. I finished my first cup of coffee and poured a second before filling Max's food and water dishes. When he eventually got up from his spot on the floor and wandered into the kitchen to eat, Emily jumped up onto the couch, circled three times, and settled in for a nap.

I sat down on the sofa next to the sleeping kitten and pulled the afghan lying over the back onto my lap. I sat and watched the fire dancing in the dark as I listened to the waves gently crashing in the background. One of the things I love most about living on the water is the steady rhythm of the waves as the tides change and the swells grow from small to large. While the fog was still as thick as pea soup, the forecast for the day was sunny and warm, so I was confident the thick cloud of moisture would dissipate as soon as the sun made its way over the horizon.

I hoped the forecast was correct because today was the community picnic and softball tournament that serve as the closing events for the three-day Founders Day celebration. In spite of the fact that I'll most certainly be sleep deprived, I'm confident that this year the Pats, the St. Patrick's Catholic Church softball team, will be victorious in the annual competition. The Pats haven't won the tournament in years, but this year, with my friend Cody West playing, I feel we have a better than average chance.

Although I'm looking forward to the day's events, I wonder how the news of Mrs. Trexler's death and Ms. Winters's arrest for her murder will affect the festivities. Both women had lived in the community their entire lives and had been well liked and highly regarded. I knew Father Kilian intended to announce the heartbreaking news to the congregation during the morning service. I imagined the overall reaction would be one of shock and despair.

And while I was concerned about how the announcement would be received, I was even more nervous about asking my Aunt Maggie the question that had been burning a hole in my soul for the past twenty hours. I hadn't been able to stop thinking about the accusation made by Ms. Winters, a woman I've known my entire life. In the process of admitting to killing Mrs. Trexler, she'd let slip a secret that I've had a hard time coming to grips with. I've tried to take the easy way out and forget what I know, but there are times in your life when unhearing what you've heard is simply impossible.

"Maybe I should go over to Maggie's early. Before Mass," I said to the kitten. "It might be easier to talk to her when she's home and no one else is around."

Emily lifted her head and yawned.

"I know. You think I should wait. But the secrecy of the whole thing has grabbed my imagination, and I'm afraid it isn't going to let go. Chances are," I continued to speak to the kitten as she climbed into my lap and began to purr, "that Ms. Winters was wrong about Maggie and I've been worrying for nothing."

The kitten closed her eyes and went back to sleep. Max jumped onto the sofa next to us as the tide began to roll in and the crashing of the waves grew louder. I pulled the afghan up over my chest and laid my head back against the sofa cushion behind me. The warmth from the fire combined with the steady rhythm of the sea lulled me into a state of relaxation. I let my mind wander to a happier time, when the entire Hart family had attended the Founders Day picnic. This year it would just be Mom, my sixteen-year-old sister Cassidy, my twenty-eight-year-old brother Danny, and me. My older sister Siobhan lives in Seattle and rarely visits, and my oldest brother, Aiden, is in Alaska fishing. My dad, who at one time had been one of the most powerful men on the island, had died in an accident almost five years ago.

I thought about how happy I was that Cody was home for the first time in ten years. I'd gotten used to him being away and rarely thought about him, but now that he'd decided to retire from the Navy and was purchasing the local newspaper, he seemed to be back in my life to stay. At first I was certain having him back wouldn't be pleasant, but in the few weeks he'd been here we'd settled into our old rhythm, and there was no doubt in my mind that our friendship was as solid as it ever had been.

At some point I must have fallen asleep because I woke to a sunny morning several hours later. I got up, made a second pot of coffee, and headed upstairs to get ready for the day. After taking a long, hot shower, I stared into my bathroom mirror and tried to work up the courage I'd somehow managed to find in the darkness of the early morning. My arms shook as I blew my thick, curly hair dry, which probably had more to do with the two pots of coffee I'd drunk than a return of my nerves.

After styling my hair and dressing in a long skirt appropriate for Mass, I checked to make sure I'd turned off the coffeepot. I refilled Emily's water and then headed toward the exterior door just off the kitchen with Max. I took a deep breath for courage as I headed across the lawn toward Maggie's much larger house. There were several ways the conversation I intended to have with my aunt could go, and I had to admit I was concerned about the eventual outcome.

I needed time to gather my thoughts, so I walked slowly, listening to the steady rhythm of the waves crashing onto the shore as I went. I tried to slow my heart rate and steady my breath as I approached the back deck. I can't remember ever being so nervous about a conversation with *anyone*. How do you ask the woman who has meant so much to you your entire life if she participated in an illicit affair with the community priest?

It was a warm morning that held the promise of an even warmer afternoon. I made a mental note to pack my shorts and tennis shoes for the picnic. I took a deep breath for courage and then slowly let it out as I climbed the four steps to Maggie's back door.

"Good morning, sweetheart. Would you like some eggs?" Maggie asked as Max and I let ourselves in through the unlocked screen door. The eggs looked wonderful, but my stomach was churning too wildly for me to eat.

"No, thank you. I need to get to the church early to get the kids ready to sing, so I only have a few minutes." I've recently taken over as co-chair of the church's children's choir with Cody.

"Something on your mind?" Maggie asked as her black cat, Akasha, wandered over to greet me.

"Actually, yes." I sat down at the dining table across from Maggie. I'd decided the best course of action was to jump right in. I never had been all that skillful at wading my way into a delicate conversation.

"When I was speaking to Ms. Winters yesterday she mentioned something that has been weighing on my mind," I continued as the gray kitten Maggie had brought home but had yet to name jumped onto the counter. "I know it's none of my business, but I can't seem to let go of the idea, so I wanted to ask you about it."

"Okay, ask away." Maggie smiled encouragingly.

I don't know why I was so nervous. Maggie lived her life like an open book. I doubted she had anything to hide.

"Ms. Winters told me that she poisoned your tea to stop you from sinning. She was under the impression that you had 'sinned' in the past; her word, not mine," I quickly added.

"Sinned?" Maggie asked.

"She believed you had acted inappropriately with certain male members of the community, and she was certain you planned to steal Toby Tillman from Patience."

"Yes, dear, you already told me that, and I've already assured everyone that any interest Toby might have in pursuing a relationship is *extremely* one-sided."

"I know that. It's just that," I paused and took a deep breath, "she indicated that you had sinned with other men in the past." I couldn't help but blush as I said the words, which had come out as more of an accusation than anything else.

Ms. Winters had confided in me while she held me at gunpoint that she had been deeply in love as a young girl, but that Maggie had stolen her man away from her, thus altering the trajectory of her entire life.

Maggie put her hands over mine as if in an offer of comfort. "I realized when you told me who had added the arsenic to my tea that Ella believed I had stolen Jason from her back in high school. But I didn't. Jason did express interest in us getting together, but at the time I was in a relationship with another boy, and I can assure you I did *nothing* to cause Jason to believe I would return his affection."

"It isn't just that." I fidgeted nervously. "Ms. Winters suggested that you sinned with Father Kilian."

Maggie sat in silence. The first thing I noticed was that she hadn't immediately denied this accusation, as she had the ones concerning Toby and Jason. The longer she sat in silence the more terrified I became. I guess that in spite of Ms. Winters's comment I hadn't *really* believed that either Maggie or Father Kilian would do such a thing.

"Father Kilian wasn't always a priest," Maggie began.

"He wasn't? What was he?"

"A child. A teenager. A young man."

"You knew him when he was young?" I asked.

"Michael was born and raised on the island, as was I. We were high school sweethearts. More than sweethearts. We planned to marry."

I wasn't expecting that. In my mind, Father Kilian had always been Father Kilian. I couldn't imagine him as anything else.

"So how did he end up a priest and you end up never marrying?" I asked.

Maggie took a sip of her coffee. I imagined she was choosing her words carefully. Sleeping with a priest, even a priest who wasn't a priest when you slept with him, would be considered quite scandalous among the more conservative residents of the island.

"Michael is the eldest son in a very traditional Catholic family that for generations held a long-standing tradition of the eldest son going into the priesthood," Maggie began. "Michael's destiny was laid out for him even before he was born. During our teenage years he had a rebellious streak, like most youth of a similar age, and vowed to live his life as he saw fit, which at the time didn't include his prechosen destiny."

"He obviously changed his mind," I said.

"Yes, he did."

I sat quietly and waited for Maggie to continue.

"I don't feel at liberty to go into detail at this time; suffice it to say that there came a point where he was forced to look at the world through the eyes of an adult rather than those of a child. He realized that his calling was so much more than *just* family custom. Michael left the island to go to seminary shortly after we graduated high school."

"And you?" I asked.

"I mourned the loss of our love, and then I made the decision to let him go and focused on building a life."

"That's so sad."

Maggie shrugged. "It was the right decision."

"But you've lived your life alone," I pointed out as the gray-and-white–striped kitten bounded into the room.

"I haven't been alone." Maggie bent down and picked up the small feline. "I've had a wonderful friendship with Marley, who's like a sister to me, and I've had you and your brothers and sisters, who feel almost like my own children. While that may not be the same thing as having a family of my own, it's enough."

I wondered if it really had been enough. I realized Maggie must have loved Father Kilian very much to choose to live her life alone after he left for the seminary. I had to wonder if he'd loved her as much. Having to make the choice between your heart and your destiny couldn't have been an easy thing to do.

"Father Kilian's cat is named Magdalene," I remembered. "Did he name her after you?"

Maggie shrugged. "Perhaps. He never said for certain, and I never asked. I have to admit I've found comfort in the idea that his naming his cat after me was Michael's way of quietly sharing with me the fact that he still cared for me. Either way, I do think it best not to point that out. There are people who wouldn't understand."

I looked at Maggie and nodded. She was, of course, correct. I could think of a handful of women who would have a heyday with the gossip that would be created by such a scandal. I wondered why Father Kilian had taken the chance in the first place. It seemed a needless risk, although few people on the island even realized that Maggie's given name was Magdalene and not Margaret.

As horrified as I was by the truth of what I'd learned, I couldn't help but let myself be swept up into the romance of the whole thing.

"Thanks for sharing this with me." I hugged Maggie. "I promise I won't tell anyone. Ever," I emphasized.

I turned to walk away, then paused at the door. "Do you think that if things had been different you and Father Kilian would have been happy together?"

Maggie smiled sadly. "I do. Very much so."

Chapter 2

"Trinity just puked in the hallway," ten-year-old Serenity Paulson informed me several hours later.

"Is she okay?" I asked as I tried to adjust the hem of Hillary Smothers's much too long choir robe.

Serenity frowned. "Of course she's not okay. I just told you, she puked."

"I realize that." I looked up from what I was doing. "I just meant . . . Oh, never mind. I'll go see how she's doing. Go tell Cody to get the mop and bucket."

I helped Hillary slip off the choir robe I was working on, then headed for the hallway. Sure enough, there was a mess for someone to clean up. Deciding it was Cody's turn to deal with the mop and bucket, I headed for the girls' bathroom. Trinity

Paulson, the youngest of the Paulson girls, was sitting on the floor crying.

"What's the matter, sweetheart?" I asked as I slid down onto the floor next to the petite girl with pale skin and long black hair.

"My stomach hurts." Trinity looked up at me with tears in her dark brown eyes. "I think I'm pregnant."

I pulled Trinity's hair back so I could see her face a little better. "I doubt that you're pregnant. You probably have the flu, or maybe you ate something that didn't agree with you. Why would you think you were pregnant?"

"Because Destiny is always puking, and I overheard her telling Cherrylynn that she thought she might be prego. Cherrylynn told her that throwing up all the time was a definite sign."

"Oh." I sighed. While I doubted eight-year-old Trinity was pregnant, it was very possible her sixteen-year-old sister, Destiny, was. Destiny was the oldest of the three sisters, and she had a wild steak her mother had been unable to tame in spite of her best efforts.

"Maybe we should call your mom and have her pick you up," I suggested.

"She's at work," Trinity sobbed. "She said she's going to get fired if she misses any more days."

"Okay, then, what about Destiny? Is she here today?"

"She's with Ricky."

Of course she was. Ricky was Destiny's boyfriend. I considered my options. I could drive Trinity home myself, but it sounded like there was no one at her house to keep an eye on her. I knew Destiny often babysat her younger siblings, but I had no idea how to get hold of the teenager.

"What time does your mom get off work?" I asked.

"Not until three. Destiny is supposed to watch me and Serenity, but she won't be back till just before Mom gets home."

"So where had you planned to go after services?" I asked. Mass was over at noon; surely the girls' mom had provided for their care until she got home.

"We was going home. Mom thinks Destiny is going to be there. Serenity can watch me."

Serenity seemed fairly mature for a twelve year old, but I hated to leave her with a sick sister. I supposed I could take Trinity into one of the unused offices and sit with her during Mass. Cody should be able to handle the choir on his own. On the other hand, if the child really was sick her mother should know.

"Do you feel well enough to move to one of the offices?" I asked.

"Yeah. I feel better." Trinity wiped her eyes with a paper towel.

"There's a sofa in Father Kilian's office. If you don't think you're going to vomit again maybe you can rest in there for a little while."

"Okay." Trinity stood up. "Don't tell no one about Destiny," she pleaded. "Mama will be mad, and Destiny will kill me for opening my trap."

"Are you sure about what you overheard?" I asked.

Trinity shrugged.

"Maybe I'll have a talk with Destiny. Just to see how she's doing," I assured the girl, who'd suddenly had a look of panic on her face.

"Don't worry; I won't tell her that you told me," I added. "Now let's get you settled."

Trinity got up from her spot on the floor and followed me down the hall to Father Kilian's office. "Will you be okay by yourself for a little while?" I asked after I'd found a blanket and got Trinity settled on the sofa.

"Yeah. I'm better now."

"I'll be just two doors down the hall if you need me. Once I get the choir ready to go I'll come back to check on you."

"Okay." The child yawned.

I had turned and headed toward the door when I noticed a photo on Father Kilian's desk. It had been taken at the church carnival the previous fall. I recognized it as one of the photos that had been taken by Orson Cobalter, the previous owner and publisher of the *Madrona Island News*. The photo featured Father Kilian, Aunt Maggie, Sister Mary, and my best friend, Tara O'Brian, standing in front of the pumpkin patch. It was a nice photo that had accompanied an article about the carnival and the community members who had pulled the whole thing together, but now that I knew what I knew, I realized for the first time that Father Kilian had his arm around Maggie, who stood to his right. Of course he also had an arm around Tara, who stood to his left, and Tara had her arm around Sister Mary, who stood on the far end, but somehow the whole thing seemed a lot less innocent than it had the first time I'd seen it.

By the time I returned to the choir room everyone was dressed in a red robe and Cody and Tara were lining the kids up based on height and vocal section.

"How's Trinity?" Tara asked as she redirected one of the altos to the alto section.

"She's feeling better. I put her down for a nap on the sofa in Father Kilian's office."

"Sister Mary said she'd go sit with her until we can arrange to have her taken home," Tara told me. "That way you can concentrate on the kids during the service."

"That's great. Thanks for filling her in on what's going on. We need to find Destiny. Trinity said her mom works until three, and Destiny is supposed to be babysitting."

"I'll go look for her once we get everyone onstage," Tara offered.

"Thanks. That would be great."

By the time Mass was over and I'd made sure all the choir kids had their robes checked in, Destiny had been located and Tara had driven all three Paulson children home. Most of the parishioners had already left for the picnic, so the church building was deserted. My car was one of only three left in the usually packed parking lot, so I couldn't help but notice the large scratch on my driver's side door. As I walked around the car for a closer look, I saw a note tucked under my windshield wiper. I was expecting it to contain an apology, along with insurance information, but when I unfolded the lined paper I found a threat instead: *Mind your own business or else.*

I looked at the scratch, which, on further examination, appeared to have been intentionally created. I briefly wondered what it was I was supposed to stay out of but decided after only a moment's thought that the threat had to be related to the mysterious case Cody and I had recently begun working on. The thing was, other than the two of us, I didn't think anyone else even knew we were looking into the decades-old incident. I folded the piece of paper and tucked it into my pants pocket. I was already late for the picnic, so I decided to consider the implications of the note when I had a bit more time.

I looked at my watch, which conveyed the fact that I was going to be late for the softball game if I didn't get a move on. I gathered my shorts and tennis shoes, then headed back into the church building so I could use the bathroom to change. I was just pulling my hair into a ponytail when I heard voices coming from the hallway. I was about to open the door to announce my presence when I heard one of them say, "I can assure you that won't be a problem," in a deep male voice.

"How can you be sure?" another man replied.

"Trust me. I'll take care of everything."

"If this is going to go smoothly we need to make certain we get the proof we need," the second man insisted.

"We'll take care of it tonight," the man with the deep voice said reassuringly.

"I keep thinking this whole thing is going to blow up in our faces."

"We've talked about this. No one is going to know. Now are you in or what?"

The pair seemed to have moved down the hall, so I was unable to hear the reply. I scooted over to the bathroom door and slowly opened it a crack. One of the men had already turned the corner, but I could see that the other one was tall with graying hair. My instinct was to follow them, although I'd need to be careful. There'd been three cars in the parking lot when I'd gone to fetch my shorts. One of them was mine, and I could only assume the other two belonged to the men I'd just overheard. If my math was correct it meant I was alone in the building with them. While their conversation might have been a lot more innocent than it seemed, I highly doubted it.

I slipped out the door and headed after them. I walked as quietly as I could, but it still sounded like my footsteps echoed in the empty corridor. When I got to the corner where I'd seen the men turn into the hallway leading out of the building, I flattened myself against the wall and slowly peeked around the corner. The hallway was empty, so I proceeded slowly.

By the time I made it out to the parking lot my car was the only vehicle left on the premises. I jogged over to my old, beat-up car and slipped into the driver's seat. I locked the doors before cranking the ignition. I'd seen enough slasher movies to know that whoever made it to the car and assumed she was safe and didn't bother with the locks was usually toast. Of course I had no idea what the men were talking about, and the odds were I was never really in any danger. Still, I couldn't silence the little voice in my head that told me those men were up to no good.

I pulled out of the parking lot and headed toward the park. As I drove along the coast road, I tried to remember everything I could about the other two vehicles. One of them had been a truck. An older model, with a lift kit. I was pretty sure it was black.

The other one had been a four-door sedan. I'm horrible at recognizing the make and model of vehicles, but I was prepared to say a newer domestic model. I did remember that it was white, which would most likely prove to be of little help because there had to be dozens of white four-door sedans on the island.

Unfortunately, I hadn't caught a license plate for either vehicle. To be honest, I'd been more focused on the scratch on my car than I had been on either of the other vehicles in the parking lot.

By the time I arrived at the park the softball teams were already warming up. I hurried over to join my team, which, by the way, won the game for the first time in years, thanks to Cody's participation

Later that evening, Cody, Danny, Tara, and I settled onto my deck to watch the sun set. It had been a long and tiring yet satisfying day. I couldn't remember the last time I'd had that much fun, in spite of the fact that the community was now mourning Mrs. Trexler's death. Having Cody as catcher to my pitching had made the softball game feel like old times. The weather had been perfect, the food delicious, and the conversation stimulating. All in all, it had been one of the best days I'd had in a long time.

The only dark spot to the day had been the fact that I'd been less than patient when I was forced to wait for the opportunity to talk to Cody about the newspaper article he'd discovered while we'd been investigating Mrs. Trexler's death. Twenty-six years ago Orson Cobalter had written a newspaper article that would have made the national news at the time, but for some reason he'd never published it. Cody and I had vowed to find out why.

"So did you get hold of Orson?" I asked when we'd all settled in with our beverage of choice.

"I got hold of his son, who told me Orson is on his way to Madrona Island to pack up his personal belongings," Cody informed us. "He should be here by tomorrow. Hopefully he'll fill in a few of the blanks."

"Wow, that worked out conveniently," I commented. "I thought you said he was just going to hire a service to pack up his house so he wouldn't have to make the trip."

"That's what he told me he planned to do when he suggested we handle the sale of the newspaper online," Cody answered. "I guess he changed his mind."

"Do you think his decision to come back to the island had anything to do with the article?" I asked.

"I doubt it, because I haven't had the opportunity to speak to him about it. I don't see how he can know I came across the article."

"Would anyone care to catch up those of us who have no idea what you're talking about?" Danny asked.

"Sorry." I glanced at Danny and Tara. "I'd forgotten we hadn't had a chance to fill you in. While we were investigating Mrs. Trexler's murder, Cody found a twenty-six-year-old newspaper article that Orson wrote and even printed but never published."

"What do you mean, never published?" Tara asked.

"There were two printings of the same edition of the *Madrona Island News*," I explained. "On the front page of the first printing, which was pulled at the last minute, there was a story about a murder on nearby Shelby Island. In the second printing, which *was* circulated, that story had been removed and replaced by an ad."

"Why would Orson do that?" Danny asked.

"That's what we'd like to know," I answered as the sap on one of the logs we were burning began to pop and crackle as it burned.

"What was in the story exactly?" Tara asked.

"The article, which, as we said, was written twenty-six years ago, claimed that Maryellen Thornton, the heiress to the Thornton millions, was living on Shelby Island with a much older man who claimed to be her husband," Cody began as Danny reached for a second beer.

"Wait," Danny stopped me. "I thought Maryellen Thornton was dead."

"That's what everyone thought happened to her, but her body was never found," I explained.

"So Orson thought she wasn't dead and that she was here? On Shelby Island?" Danny clarified.

"That's what was in the article," I said.

"Wow, I remember hearing about that in school," Tara responded. "The Thornton family weren't just worth millions, they were worth hundreds of millions, which was a *lot* of money back then."

"Hundreds of millions is a lot of money now," I countered, "but I get your point. The family wasn't just rich, they were crazy rich."

"Why do you think Orson cut the story?" Tara asked.

"We aren't sure," Cody admitted. "The article outlined a pretty complex set of circumstances, so if I had to guess, I'd say that perhaps he realized he'd made a mistake and pulled the story at the last minute."

"What did the article say exactly?" Danny asked. I could see he was completely pulled into the mystery.

"Orson started off by providing a bit of background about the original kidnapping," Cody began. "In case you aren't familiar with the case, it seemed the couple's housekeeper found Mr. and Mrs. Thornton dead in the upstairs hallway of their mansion when she came to do the daily cleaning. Maryellen's body wasn't on the premises, and initially it was believed that she'd been kidnapped, but there was never a ransom demand, and the girl was never seen or heard from again, in spite of a massive search conducted over more than a year. At some point one of Mr. Thornton's siblings had Maryellen declared legally dead so the estate could be settled."

"Wow. If she actually was alive ten years after she went missing, her claim to the money would create quite a mess," Tara stated.

Cody nodded. "I guess it would, although if the entire story is accurate her state of undeadness might not have been an issue. The article ended by accusing her of murder."

"She killed someone?" Tara gasped.

"If the article is to be believed," Cody confirmed.

"Who?" Tara asked.

"Let me back up," Cody suggested. "While the article was focused on the murder of the woman's husband, the notes, which Orson compiled in a journal, tell a much fuller story. According to the journal, Orson was living on Shelby Island at the time of the man's death. Shelby Island was inhabited by only a handful of families and Orson, as well as Jim and Jane Farmington, were the only two residents of the isolated west shore."

"So they were neighbors," Danny clarified.

"They were," Cody confirmed. "Orson's notes indicate that when the couple first moved to the island

Jane was pregnant and well into her final trimester. Although the couple liked to keep to themselves, when Orson noticed the woman in the yard a month or so after they'd moved in, he stopped to congratulate her and inquire about the baby because she must have delivered. The woman, who refused to look him in the eye, told Orson that the baby—a girl—had died at birth. Orson offered his condolences and went on his way, but there was something about the girl's story that didn't seem right, so he decided to look into it further. Upon investigation, he found nothing."

"Nothing?" Tara asked.

"Not only wasn't there a record of the baby's birth, there also wasn't a record of the baby's death."

"So she lied," Danny guessed.

"It seems likely. Several weeks later," Cody continued, "Orson wrote in his journal that he saw the girl in the yard again, and again he stopped to chat. He noticed that the girl had a black eye and a swollen cheek. He asked her if someone had hit her, and she told him she had fallen and hit her face on a rock. When he asked about the baby and the lack of records, the woman told him that she'd had a home birth and that the baby was buried in the yard. Orson suspected the woman was a battered wife. It seemed obvious that Jane was afraid of Jim. Not only did she tend to act skittish and avoid eye contact when Orson spoke to her, but he wrote that he had never seen her leave the confines of the property the couple owned in all the months they'd lived there. He decided to investigate further, so he snuck onto the property one evening when Jim was away and Jane was busy indoors. He noted in the journal that in spite of a fairly careful search he couldn't find any sign of a grave or any evidence that the earth had been disturbed anywhere."

"So what happened to the baby?" Tara asked.

"Orson didn't know, but his curiosity had been piqued, so he began to do some investigating. It was his theory that the child might have been sold."

"Sold?" Tara questioned.

"The baby was missing, there was no evidence of a grave, and the girl was obviously being abused. Additionally, the husband never left the island to go to work, yet they seemed to have money. Orson had recently read an article about the money that could be made via black market adoptions and developed a theory based on his observations. It was during his research into missing children that he came across a photo of Maryellen Thornton and realized that Jane looked an awful lot like the missing girl."

"He must have been shocked," Danny said.

"I don't know whether he was shocked," Cody responded, "but he was intrigued enough to keep looking. He must have decided at some point that he had enough to alert the local sheriff, because he made a note about having done so. The problem was that he had nothing to go on but speculation, and Jane swore she wasn't Maryellen and that her baby really had died. When she was asked to point out the baby's grave she revealed that Jim had thought it best to bury the baby at sea."

"Oh, no, that doesn't sound suspicious at all," I said sarcastically.

"Orson was even more convinced at that point that something suspicious was going on," Cody continued. "He tried alerting Maryellen's family that it was possible she was alive, but a representative stated that Maryellen had been declared legally dead and was unwilling to dig up the past and upset everyone."

"Of course the family didn't want to dig up the past," Danny commented. "Who knows what that might have meant for everyone's inheritance?"

"Exactly," Cody agreed. "That was when, as far as I can tell, that Orson began to write his article. I think he figured if he made it public that Maryellen Thornton might still be alive the family would have no choice but to look into it. The notes became sketchy at that point, so I'm uncertain exactly what occurred. I found a rough draft of the article that stated his belief that Maryellen Thornton was alive and living on Shelby Island. The rough draft ended with that assertion alone. The article that was printed but not circulated, however, added that Maryellen was a battered wife and had ended her torture by killing her abusive husband in self-defense."

"The poor thing," I sympathized.

"Here's the strange thing," Cody said, and paused.

I could feel the heat from the fire on my face as I waited for Cody to continue. He took a sip of his beer, I assumed to wet his throat, or possibly to build suspense, before finishing the story.

"I spoke to Finn at church this morning," Cody told them. "He promised to look into the death of Jim Farmington. He called me this afternoon and said he couldn't find any record of the man having been murdered, so he called Tripp Brimmer, who's retired now but was the resident deputy on Madrona Island before Finn was hired. Tripp confirmed that there was never a murder on Shelby Island. The couple simply moved away. Finn checked into the county records and confirmed that there's no record of Jim Farmington's death here."

I frowned. "Okay, that *is* strange. Why would Orson write an article that claimed Jane Farmington, who he believed was really Maryellen Thornton, had killed her husband in self-defense if the man hadn't actually died?"

"I have no idea." Cody shrugged. "I'm hoping he can answer that question when we meet tomorrow."

"Unless Orson knows a lot more than he indicated in his notes, it's going to be hard to investigate a mystery this old," Danny commented. "Especially when no one who seems to have been involved even lives in the area any longer."

"Yeah, it's a long shot," Cody admitted. "If Orson doesn't have more to contribute, we're probably looking at a dead end."

Emily came out onto the deck through the open door and climbed into Tara's lap next to her kitten, Bandit, who was already napping there. "I see you have a new houseguest," Tara said.

"Tara, meet Emily; Emily, Tara."

"She's cute. Where did you find her?" Tara asked.

"At my front door. The house was chanting her name."

"The house was chanting her name?" Danny questioned.

I explained about being awakened by the dripping faucet, despite the fact that none of my faucets were dripping.

"Have you asked Tansy about her?" Tara asked.

"I haven't had a chance, but I thought I'd stop by to talk to her tomorrow. Emily's strange appearance definitely seems like a Tansy thing."

"Maybe Emily is here to help with the mystery Orson was working on," Tara suggested.

Danny laughed. "That itty-bitty thing is going to solve a mystery that has a bunch of adults, including the sheriff, stumped?"

"Stranger things have happened lately," Tara pointed out.

"Tara's right," I defended my best friend. "I'm almost certain Emily is here for a specific purpose. I just don't know what it is yet."

"Okay, kitty," Danny said sarcastically, "what do you have for us?"

Emily leaped out of Tara's lap and pounced on Danny's arm, causing him to dump his beer down the front of his shirt. Everyone, including Danny, laughed.

"Okay, I give." Danny held up his hands in surrender.

"I have a couple of shirts you've left here on various occasions. I'll get one," I offered,

Emily followed me as I went inside to search for one of Danny's forgotten shirts. She ran up the stairs in front of me before jumping on my bed, which she used as a launching point to get onto my dresser. She batted around the loose objects I had on the top while

I weeded through my closet. When I heard a crash I grimaced. I was going to have to keep my things picked up now that I had a kitten in the house. I grabbed one of Danny's shirts, then turned to see what the kitten had knocked over. Lying on the floor was a book I had dug out for Haley, the girl who was helping out at the cat sanctuary for the summer, an old copy of *Grimm's Fairy Tales*. I wasn't certain what a book of fairy tales had to do with a decades-old murder mystery, but if Tansy *had* sent Emily, then chances were the book would somehow contain a clue.

Chapter 3

Monday, June 8

The next morning I got up early so Max and I could take a run on the beach before I had to head into town to help Tara with the remodel of Coffee Cat Books. I love the early morning, when the beach is deserted except for a few fishermen and the seagulls that circle overhead, looking for scraps. The sun rises early during the summer in this part of the country, so, although the bright yellow ball of energy had already begun its ascent, it was still hours before most of the island would awaken.

Max splashed in the waves as I settled into a steady rhythm. I focused on my breath as I watched the waves roll onto the shore ahead of me, only to retreat back into the sea. A lot of the families that had lived on the island when I was growing up had moved on with the changes in fishing regulations, but I knew in my heart that no matter what else might happen, I would live out my life on the island where I was born.

I slowed as I began to climb the dunes that had formed at the south end of the beach. The higher I climbed, the farther I could see into the horizon. A pair of gray whales were frolicking in the distance as an early morning tour boat trolled alongside. The boat didn't look like Danny's, but I was willing to bet he'd be out on a morning as clear as this. I paused as I reached the top of the dune. I closed my eyes and listened to the waves crashing below as the chilly morning air cooled my face. Max sat in the sand next to me as we took a minute to give thanks for all we had.

As we continued on toward Pelican Bay, I decided to stop in to say hi to Banjo and Summer, a hippie couple who owned a shack on the beach just outside of town. It was hard to know if they'd be up and about at this time of day, but Summer had called me while I was in Harthaven the day before to inform me that one of the feral cats that lived on their property had had kittens. One of the goals of Harthaven Cat Sanctuary is to round up all the feral kittens early enough to socialize them so that they're eligible for forever homes. Adult cats are neutered or spayed and then housed in the sanctuary until they're ready for homes of their own. Some cats never are able to be domesticated, but we do what we can to keep them safe and comfortable and away from people like Mayor Bradley, who would prefer to have them destroyed.

As I rounded the corner, I could see that both Banjo and Summer were in the middle of their morning yoga. It appeared they had developed a well-orchestrated routine as they flowingly moved from one post to the next. I'd tried yoga a few times, but I wasn't nearly as graceful as the couple practicing on the beach. I sat silently and waited for them to finish. Max sat down next to me on the sand. There was something so serene about watching the graceful routine orchestrated effortlessly on the white sand bordering the gently rolling sea. There are those who might look at Banjo and Summer and wonder why they lived as sparsely as they did, but you need only watch the serenity and contentment on their faces to realize they lived exactly the life they yearned for.

"Cait, have you been here long?" Summer asked after their routine had come to an end.

"Not long. Max and I were out for a run and decided to stop by to check on the kittens you called me about."

"The mama cat made a nest behind the rocks over there." Summer pointed her slim and tanned arm toward a point just beyond the dune by a rock formation. "As far as locations go, it isn't bad. It's protected and away from the tide, but I know you like to domesticate those you can."

"I'm afraid that ever since Mayor Bradley passed the law making it legal to remove cats from your property by any means necessary, cats are no longer safe in the wild. I'll come back later with Haley. She seems to have a way with even the orneriest cats."

"That girl is really something special," Summer agreed. "She has a calming way about her."

"Yeah, she's really been a godsend. I'll miss her when she leaves at the end of the season. She even has Moose eating out of her hand." Moose was a lifer at Harthaven Cat Sanctuary due to his distrust and dislike of almost all humans.

"I should be around this morning," Summer informed me. "Just come over and knock on my door when you get back and I'll help you round everyone up. It's going to be important to get the mama because the babies are so young."

"I'll bring the traps I need. Thanks for calling when you did. The younger they are when we get them, the more likely they are to find homes. I'm sure we'll be able to find wonderful placements for the kittens when they're old enough to be weaned."

"Do you think you can bring the mama back?" Summer asked. "She tends to hang out on our property because we feed her, and I've gotten used to having her around."

"If you think she'll stay on your property and out of danger, I think that can be arranged."

"I think we have an understanding," Summer assured me.

"Okay, great. Once the kittens are weaned we'll spay the mama to avoid another litter and I'll bring her back to you. I'll see you in a couple of hours."

I left Summer and continued on into town. I'd decided I really did need to verify that Tansy had sent Emily and I wasn't just imagining the whole thing. As I jogged along Main Street, which runs parallel to the harbor, I waved to the various business owners who were out and about, beginning their tasks of setting up for the hordes of tourists who come to the island on the ferry during the warmer summer months.

I crossed Main and headed over to the street where Bella and Tansy shared a house. I always enjoy visiting the two women who many claim are witches and others think are just unusually perceptive. Neither Bella nor Tansy seem to be willing to verify or deny the label, but I do know that if you're trying to make sense of something that on the surface makes no sense, these two women are the ones to speak to.

"Good morning," I greeted the pair, who were sitting on their front porch sipping their morning tea.

"Good morning to you, Cait," Bella greeted. "And you as well, Max."

I let myself in through the front gate and walked up the rose-lined path that ran from the sidewalk to the porch. I sat down on one of the vacant chairs while Max made himself at home on the cool grass, which was still partially shaded.

"Did Emily find you okay?" Tansy asked.

"She did. Which is why I decided to stop by. I wanted to make sure I wasn't imagining things." I looked directly at the woman. "I know this is going to sound odd, but the house seemed to be chanting her name. Or at least it seemed like the drip, drip, drip of the faucet was whispering 'Emily, Emily, Emily.'"

"I don't find that strange at all." Tansy smiled. "Would you like some of the whole-grain bread Bella baked this morning?"

"The bread looks delicious, but I really should get home. I need to help Maggie with the cats, and I promised Summer I'd go there to pick up some of the feral cats living on her property."

"I'll send a loaf home with you," Bella offered.

"Thanks. That would be nice. I'll share it with Maggie."

Bella got up from her chair and went inside to fetch the bread. It seemed that every time I dropped in on Bella and Tansy I ended up taking some type of bread, muffin, or pastry home.

"Is Maggie doing better now that she's no longer drinking tainted tea?" Tansy asked.

"Yes, she's doing a lot better. It won't be long before she's back to her old self."

"I'm so glad. She'll need her strength for the challenges ahead."

I didn't want to know what she meant by that. If Tansy said it you could bet it would turn out to be true, but the only message I got from the statement was that there were hard times ahead. To be honest, I was ready for a break from the hard times we'd been working through as of late.

"I'm guessing you must somehow know about the old murder mystery Cody and I are looking in to," I stated. "And that's why you sent Emily."

Tansy shrugged. "There are many things you're destined to find and many things you're destined to know. Just remember, with knowing comes a burden that, at times, is best carried alone."

I frowned. "A burden? What burden?"

Tansy looked up toward the house. "Bella is coming with your bread. It's been nice visiting, but you don't want be late."

"Late? For what?"

Tansy smiled, stood up, and headed inside.

I went home, showered and changed, played with Emily, picked up Haley and successfully rounded up both mother and kittens, turned Haley over to

Maggie, and then headed into town on my bike. I was going to be late arriving at Coffee Cat Books. Again. Maybe that was what Tansy had been referring to when she indicated that I'd be late. It seemed that no matter how hard I tried I just couldn't seem to be the partner Tara deserved. Not that she complained. Tara was great. She was efficient and organized and probably didn't even need my help, but she had gone out of her way to make me feel a real part of the project in spite of the fact that I hadn't been upholding my end of the deal.

At least I hadn't been holding up my end of the deal to this point. Today, I vowed, I would work my hiney off to make up for all the work I'd missed. I peddled faster as I rode along the dirt trail that paralleled the ocean. It was a narrow but hard-packed trail that was perfect for biking despite the fact that it was utilized by only a few locals. I wasn't complaining. I enjoyed the fact that most mornings mine was the only bike to travel the isolated but scenic trail.

The path was usually free of clutter during the summer months and I found I was making good time. I might even have arrived at Coffee Cat Books at the promised hour if I hadn't seen a pair of sneakers abandoned on the side of the trail. I slowed down to give them a closer look and realized that the sneakers I'd seen weren't actually abandoned at all.

"Oh, great." I sighed as I slowed my bike. The mostly buried body was obviously male based on the ginormous size of the tennis shoes that had caught my attention in the first place. Fine grains of sand covered most of the body, but I did notice a blue and white T-shirt and the bill of what looked a lot like a Seattle Seahawks cap.

I laid my bike in the sand and called Finn, hoping he'd answer. I knew from previous experience that Finn would have a cow if I so much as touched a single grain of the sand covering the man, but somehow it felt wrong to just leave him lying there like that. The sun was climbing in the sky and before long the body, which was now in the shade of a dune, would be baking in the summer sun.

After I spoke to Finn I called Cody. It might seem odd that he's the person I would turn to in a time of crisis, but in the short time he's been back on the island we've bonded over a shared interest in solving murders and sticking our noses into other mysteries that are probably none of our business. I trusted Cody and knew he was a good person to have around in a crisis. He was smart and levelheaded and seemed to know just what to do in almost any circumstance.

Once Cody assured me he was on his way as well, I called Tara to inform her that, once again, I'd be late. She assured me it was fine; that I should take all the time I needed and let her know if I needed her help for anything.

I sat down on a nearby rock to wait, trying to imagine who might be buried under the sand. I could tell the man was tall and probably a local, based on the cap from the area's favorite team. I couldn't tell how long the man had been dead, but while the trail I traveled wasn't popular among visitors, it was a route that was used by locals from time to time. It was still early, so my best guess was that the man had been buried in the sand at some point during the night.

I glanced out at the open sea and tried to ignore the body behind me. There was a part of me that could barely resist the urge to remove the sand from the man's face at a minimum. How awful to have sand in your eyes and mouth, even if you were dead. I felt a tear run down my cheek as the reality of what had occurred hit me. Chances were, once the man was unmasked, it was going to be someone I knew, perhaps someone I cared about. While it was possible the man was a visitor to our island, my intuition told me otherwise.

I couldn't believe we'd had another murder on the island. We'd only just buried Keith Weaver a short time ago, and the funeral for Mrs. Trexler was scheduled for the following morning. On an island the size of Madrona, you'd think you'd have time to bury one murder victim before discovering another.

"Sorry it took me so long to get here." Cody jogged up and knelt down in the sand beside me. "I had to make sure Mr. Parsons was okay before I left."

I wrapped my arms around Cody's neck and sobbed into his shirt.

"Is it someone you know?" Cody asked.

"I don't know."

"Then why are you crying?"

"I don't know."

I could feel Cody glancing toward the body over my shoulder. "Are you sure he's dead?"

God, I hoped so. I hadn't even thought to check for a pulse. The man had looked dead, and I was pretty sure he hadn't moved in the time I'd been waiting there. I lifted my head. "Should we check?"

Cody stood up. "I'll do it. You wait here."

I watched as Cody walked over to the man and uncovered just enough of his head to check for a pulse. He looked back toward me. "It's Orson."

"Orson?" I asked as Finn pulled up in his four-wheel-drive truck.

He got out of the truck and pulled on a pair of gloves. I watched from a distance as he checked for a pulse, then began to remove the sand from the victim's face.

"What happened?" I asked as Finn removed a bit more of the sand and carefully rolled the man to his side.

"Hit on the head with a blunt object," Finn informed us. "I'd better call over to the main office so they can send a team."

Finn was the resident deputy on Madrona Island. The sheriff, as well as the only jail in the area, was housed at the county seat. Finn was well equipped to handle the day-to-day petty crimes that seemed to find their way into every community, but in circumstances such as a dead body, a team would most likely be sent over from the mainland.

Finn made his calls and then asked Cody to help him surround the area with yellow tape, while I stayed where I was and waited. I knew the man beneath the sand was Orson—both Finn and Cody had said as much—but somehow my mind refused to process that piece of information.

What were the odds that Orson would end up dead virtually the instant he returned to the island and the day after Cody began asking questions about a long-forgotten and never-published article, before he'd even had a chance to meet with us?

Zero.

"You know this has to be the result of our snooping around in that old case," I asserted.

"Probably," Finn agreed.

"Which means that the case isn't as cold as we originally thought," Cody added.

"Yeah, but other than the three of us, Danny, and Tara, who even knows we found the article?" I asked.

Finn frowned. "I did nose around in the county files looking for a record of Jim Farmington's death. When we log into the county system it creates a record of everything we look at. The county offices were closed yesterday, though, so it isn't likely anyone would have had the opportunity to look at the log until this morning. It looks like Orson has been dead at least eight hours, so I doubt my inquiry had anything to do with his murder."

"Is it possible to set up an alert?" I asked.

Finn's eyes widened. "Yes, actually, it is. If someone has the right clearance and they're interested in finding out who might be looking at a specific file, they can set up an alert that texts them whenever anyone accesses it."

"Is there a way to find out who might have set up an alert for the files you accessed?" I wondered.

"It depends on the security level of the person establishing it. I'll look into it as soon as I finish with the crime scene guys."

I watched as Cody and Finn finished securing the area. I realized that I should be concerned about how familiar I was becoming with the process. I really did need to stop finding bodies everywhere I went. I was beginning to feel like I was in some way linked to all the tragedy the island had seen during the past month.

When the men were finished with what they were doing Cody walked back over and hugged me. I let myself sink into his body. I was an independent sort who normally wouldn't welcome being taken care of, but in this instance I was happy to have Cody's strength to lean on.

"Do you need us to stay?" Cody asked Finn after he'd returned his supplies to his truck.

"No. I'll call you or come by if I need additional information."

I continued on to Coffee Cat Books and Cody returned to Mr. Parsons's to see to his breakfast. We arranged to get together later in the afternoon to discuss Madrona Island's most recent murder. Cody was planning to head over to the newspaper after making sure that Mr. Parsons was comfortable, so I agreed to stop by when the opportunity presented itself.

In spite of the fact that I seemed to be continually bailing on Tara, I really was excited about Coffee Cat Books. The amount of work that had been done in such a short period of time was remarkable. The new walls were in, as were the new windows that opened up the space so it felt like the harbor flowed into the room. I could imagine sitting next to the huge picture windows as the various seasons passed by. Sailboats would be coming and going in the harbor during the summer months, and it would be awesome to watch dark storms blow in from the west during the winter months. On those occasions when it snowed, it would be like viewing the world from inside a snow globe.

The centerpiece of the cat room was a huge floor-to-ceiling fireplace that was framed on each side by yet another wall of windows. I figured we'd be busy even during the winter months. I couldn't imagine anyone would be able to resist curling up on one of our sofas with a good book, a cup of coffee or tea, and a kitty curled up in their lap. I closed my eyes and imagined the feeling of warmth and security the bookstore would provide as winter storms raged outside.

I opened my eyes and looked around the room. The old flooring had been torn out and the new one was scheduled to be installed in a week or two. Then we'd be able to begin installing the interior shelving and displays. The building was located on the wharf, where the ferry docked four times every day, so Tara and I were counting on foot traffic to make up most of our customer base.

In addition to selling coffee and coffee beverages at the coffee bar, we also planned to carry a variety of juice and water offerings. Tara wanted to feature a different pastry every day, and I hoped for both indoor and outdoor seating during the warmer months.

Tara and I had already ordered a good selection of books and book-related gifts. Inventory is a tricky thing, and Tara felt it best that we start off slow and then continue to add as funding allowed. I'm sure both locals and visitors from the mainland will want to order a cup of coffee, buy a book, and curl up next to one of the adoptable cats we plan to feature.

"So you found another body?" Tara whispered after she joined me.

"It was Orson," I whispered in return.

"Orson? Really? You don't think . . . ?"

"Actually, I do. It just would be too strange if Orson was killed for any other reason. He lived here for decades. People liked him. His death has to do with our snooping around in that old mystery. I was interested in it before, but now I feel like we owe it to him to find the truth. I'm going to meet up with Cody this afternoon to discuss a strategy."

"I'm fine here," Tara assured me. "You go ahead and do what you need to do."

"Are we still on for *Cooking With Cathy* tonight?" I asked.

Tara and I are closet foodies. Every Monday evening, without fail, we watch *Cooking With Cathy*. Not only do we make the delicious offerings along with Cathy but we share a bottle of wine and sample our efforts as well.

"Unless you get tied up," Tara answered.

"I'll call you later. Why don't you plan to come by either way and we can catch up?"

I hung around for a while longer and pretended I was helping, but Tara really did have everything under control. Tara is not only überefficient but she's a take-charge sort of person who knows what she wants and how to get it. Me? I tend to be a bit more kickback. Some would say *too* kickback. I like to go with the flow and see where life takes me, while Tara likes to pick out the vehicle, choose the path, and do the driving.

Still, Tara is my very best friend in the world, and despite the fact that we tend to be very different we somehow manage to make a good team. I oftentimes look back on my life and realize that I would be a very different person without her steady influence.

By the time I reached the still-closed office of the *Madrona Island News*, Cody was already there. He sat at the table we'd often used to do research with a pile of old newspapers in front of him. I hated to admit it, but he looked more defeated than I had ever seen him. I guess I could understand why. It seemed very likely that Orson had died because of our actions in a situation that was really none of our business.

"Do you think we should continue with this?" I asked after I'd sat down next to him.

Cody looked at me. "Maybe we shouldn't, but at this point I'm not sure I can let it go."

"Yeah, me neither. Any idea what we should do next?" I asked.

"Honestly? Not a clue."

Chapter 4

In a world that seemed to be spinning out of control there was something grounding about the predictability of joining Tara to cook alongside *Cooking With Cathy*. Tara and I had been spending every Monday evening with the show for more than four years. Tonight we were making a spicy Mexican lasagna that looked like it was going to taste wonderful. The recipe called for precooked and shredded or diced chicken breasts, which I'd gone home early to prepare. I'd also pregrated the cheese so that all we'd need to do was assemble the delicious offering. We planned to serve it to Cody and Danny, who'd promised to stop by at about the time the show ended.

In addition to the creamy lasagna we planned to serve warm tortilla chips, homemade salsa, and refreshing margaritas with fresh-squeezed lime. After the stressful day I'd had, an evening of food with friends seemed exactly the diversion I needed.

"I wonder if you can replace the ricotta with cottage cheese?" Tara said.

"I don't see why not. In fact, as long as the overall consistency remains the same, I don't see why you can't replace any of the ingredients with others. Personally, I think the sauce would be good if you added a bit of chili powder. Or maybe even horseradish."

"Do you have any horseradish?" Tara asked.

"No. But I might try making this again with a few substitutions. I bet it would be good with spicy shredded beef instead of chicken. Maybe we can try that the next time we have friends over for dinner."

"Which seems like that's practically every night lately," Tara joked.

Tara wasn't wrong. With all the murder investigations we'd been involved in lately it did seem like we'd had Danny and Cody over for dinner more often than not.

"This investigation has me spooked a lot more than the others we've dealt with."

"Spooked how?" Tara asked as she slid the casserole into the oven.

"For one thing, the only possible motive I can come up with for Orson's murder is that someone found out that Cody and I were asking around about his investigation twenty-six years ago. That makes me wonder if the rest of us are in some sort of danger. For another thing, Tansy made an odd comment today that led me to believe that even if we find the answers we're seeking, we might end up wishing we never found out whatever it is we seemed destined to find out."

"*Destined* seems like a strong word," Tara stated.

"I guess I might be taking this a lot more personally than I really should," I admitted.

"You could always drop it if it gets too intense."

I shrugged. "Yeah, maybe. But now that Orson's dead and it's most likely because of our snooping, Cody and I sort of feel like it's our responsibility to see this through."

Tara picked up a piece of cheese and nibbled on the end, then leaned against the counter and looked at me. "If you think there's any real danger maybe you *should* drop it before someone else ends up dead. Have you asked Finn what he thinks?"

"He wants us to stay out of it. He always wants us to stay out of it," I emphasized. "And maybe we should. I just have a feeling that in this case Cody won't. He really seems committed to figuring this out, and if he's in, I'm in."

"You and Cody seem to be spending a lot of time together," Tara observed. "Is there something more going on than the rekindling of an old friendship?"

Was there? I wasn't sure. But my response was more assured than I felt. "No, not at all. We just seem to keep getting thrown into these intense situations together."

"Did you get any closer to finding the answers you were looking for this afternoon?"

"No, not really. Cody wanted to follow up on a few things after I left, so maybe he'll know more when he gets here."

I began rinsing the dishes we'd used while Tara put away the extra ingredients we hadn't. We worked in comfortable silence until the kitchen was clean, each lost in our own thoughts.

"Should we make something for dessert?" Tara asked. Leave it to sweet-tooth Tara to bring up dessert.

"Something like ice cream would taste good after a heavy, spicy meal," I suggested.

"How about a parfait with sherbet and fresh berries?"

"Sounds—yikes!" I shouted as Emily and Tara's kitten Bandit came charging through the kitchen like furry wrecking balls.

"Boy, are they wound up." Tara laughed as I tried to right myself after almost tripping on the dynamic duo as they circled around the table and headed back up the stairs.

"They really are having the best time." I cringed as I heard a crash overhead. "I guess I should see what they destroyed."

"I'll run to the store to get what we need to make the dessert. Do you need anything else?"

"No, I think we're set."

After Tara left I headed upstairs to see what the kittens had knocked over. One of my potted plants was lying on its side, half the dirt, which at one time had covered the root ball, scattered across the floor. A tube of lip gloss was tucked inside one of my tennis shoes and I was certain the pillow that used to sit on my bed was going to need to be recovered.

"How in the world did the two of you manage to make such a huge mess in such a short amount of time?" I groaned.

Both kittens jumped up onto the bed, where they sat watching as I attempted to right the room. I supposed there hadn't been any real damage, but I could see I was going to need to keep a closer eye on the dastardly duo when they were together. I picked up the copy of *Grimm's Fairy Tales*, which had been knocked to the floor again. I'd forgotten I'd meant to go back to see if there was something about the book that stood out as relevant. I opened the hardback cover and thumbed through the pages. Nothing jumped out at me. Emily was pretty young; maybe she hadn't yet had time to come into her own as a co-sleuth.

I was about to set the book aside when I noticed a piece of paper tucked into the middle of it. At first I thought the paper might tell me something, but it turned out to be blank, probably just something that had been used as a bookmark. I tossed the paper aside and was about to close the book when I noticed the fairy tale the paper had been marking was *The Gold-Children*. Coincidence? I doubted it.

I read the fairy tale, which told of a poor fisherman who one day pulled a golden fish out of the water. The fish promised the fisherman a great castle if he would throw him back. The fisherman agreed and the man's hut was transformed into a castle. Each time the man caught the fish it made a similar offer, until the man had all the wealth he would ever need.

I looked at Emily, who was using one paw to clean her face. "I don't suppose you're trying to tell me that I'm about to come into great wealth?"

The cat ignored me.

"No. I didn't think so."

Emily looked at me one last time and then curled up on the bed with Bandit. Both kittens fell into an exhausted sleep. The moral of the story? I had a feeling that at some point I'd find out.

Later, we settled onto the front deck to enjoy our dinner and watch the sun set into the peaceful sea. The moon was waxing and looked to be nearing its journey from new to full. I hadn't been following the charts, but if I had to guess it would be full sometime before the weekend.

There's something so serene about a full moon reflecting off a calm sea. When the air is warm and still and stars decorate the night sky, it's almost possible to feel an integral part of the vastness of the universe surrounding you. I closed my eyes and listened as the waves gently lapped onto the shore. Danny and Cody had offered to do the dishes, and Tara was inside making sure the kittens were behaving themselves. I'm not sure I'd really stopped to breathe since the moment I found Orson buried in the sand.

I'd played over and over again in my mind the possible sequence of events that might have led to the man's death. It was hard to imagine anyone who could have known what we were up to would have killed him. Cody and I had talked about it. I'd mentioned the newspaper article briefly to Maggie, and we'd filled Finn in on our findings. We'd discussed the case with Danny and Tara, but based on the official time of death, it seemed likely that Orson was already dead before we shared the story with our best friends. Finn had admitted it was possible for someone to flag a file, but only those with high clearance were able to do so, which would mean that if Orson had been killed due to a file being flagged, the killer had to be someone with unrestricted access to county records.

The whole thing made no sense.

"Are you sleeping?" Cody asked.

"Um," I answered without opening my eyes.

"Would you like us to leave?"

I opened my eyes and sat up in my chair. "Don't go. I was just thinking about Orson and trying to figure out who could possibly be placed on a suspect list."

"There don't seem to be many likely candidates," Cody admitted as he tossed a couple of extra logs on the fire we'd built.

"I called Finn earlier and he said he'd try to stop by, but he's been swamped all day. Maybe he'll get a lead on Orson's killer. It's possible his death isn't connected to that old mystery we've been digging around in. Admittedly it's unlikely he was killed for some other reason but not impossible."

Cody sat down next to me and took my hand, weaving his fingers through mine. We sat quietly while we waited for Danny and Tara to join us. It felt so natural for us to find comfort in each other. I had a hard time believing Cody had been back on Madrona Island for less than four weeks. In some ways it felt like he'd never left.

By the time Finn arrived the rest of us were about ready to call it a night, but it seemed rude not to listen to what he had to say, so I reheated some of the Mexican lasagna and Tara made him a drink. The poor guy had been so busy he hadn't had a chance to eat all day.

"So what do we know?" I asked Finn after he'd finished his meal.

"As I thought, Orson died as a result of blunt force trauma to the head. While it's likely he was hit by a heavy object, the location of the wound suggests it's possible he fell and hit his head on something like a rock or something else."

"If he fell he wouldn't have been buried in the sand," I pointed out.

"Orson didn't die at the location where you found him," Finn informed me. "We've determined that he was killed and bled out somewhere else because there was no blood found at the beach."

"Why would someone move him if he simply fell and hit his head?" Cody asked.

"It's unlikely anyone would, which is why we believe he was murdered. Still, right now we can't rule out an accident."

"It seems odd to me," I began, "that someone went to all the trouble to move the body but then left him just off the bike trail. The place he was left assured that he would be found. Why move the body if not to hide it?"

"Good question," Finn agreed.

"Do we know when he arrived on the island?" Cody asked.

"I checked with the guys who were working the ferry yesterday, and they all agreed that Orson arrived on the five-thirty ferry. The medical examiner puts the time of death between nine and ten, which means that he hadn't been on the island long before whatever happened occurred. There was a pile of mail just inside the front door of his house where it had been deposited through the slot. That leads me to believe that Orson never did make it home. Chances are he arrived on the island around dinnertime, realized that he didn't have groceries, and went to get something to eat. I have some feelers out to local restaurants, but so far no one has admitted to having seen him. Did you know Orson was coming to the island prior to calling and speaking to his brother?" Finn asked Cody.

"No. He never told me he was going to make the trip out. In fact, he seemed to indicate that we would complete the sale of the newspaper via emails and bank transfers. I was as surprised as anyone when I called him to ask about the article and found out he was on his way west."

"I wonder if he decided to come to the island because we found the article," I asked.

Finn shrugged. "It seems as likely as anything. Maybe there was something he needed to clean up or someone he needed to warn."

"Wait a minute," Cody halted the conversation. "Orson would have had to have left for Madrona Island before I called to speak to him. How would he have known I'd even found the article?"

"I guess someone who knew he kept the uncirculated newspaper could have called to remind him of the information that was revealed once they realized he was selling the newspaper," Finn theorized. "Maybe once he realized what the article revealed he also realized he needed to warn someone."

"If he wanted to warn someone that we might find the article and decide to snoop around in the mystery he could have just called them," I pointed out. "Have you looked at phone records?"

"I have. If he called someone he didn't use his own phone."

"You know, it seems like there's a lot of theorizing going on here," Tara said, "but we're desperately short on facts. For all we know, Orson came to Madrona Island for a reason that had nothing to do with the newspaper article. I think if you focus on that one fact too exclusively you might miss another more realistic motive."

"Tara's right," Danny agreed.

"If he was murdered, maybe we can flush out the killer by leaking a rumor that we have a lead and then see if anyone acts on it," I suggested.

Finn frowned at me. "I'm pretty sure that only works on TV. Besides, I really want you," he looked around at the group, "all of you, to let me handle this. If someone did kill Orson to cover up a secret, it's a good bet that person would be willing to kill again if need be."

Finn looked directly at me. "Promise me."

I looked at the others and could see they all seemed to agree with Finn.

"Okay. I promise."

Chapter 5

Tuesday June 9

I woke to the sound of rain hitting the roof of my cabin. The gloomy weather was appropriate for the occasion, but I knew it wouldn't be welcome by most. Today the community would gather to say good-bye to Susan Trexler, a woman who had taught third grade to island children for decades before retiring a few years back. Mrs. Trexler had been liked and respected by most in the tight-knit community, but I knew, as did a few others, that although she'd spent her life in public service, she'd died with a secret.

I leaned on one elbow to assess the situation. Emily was sleeping under the covers with her head leaning against my left thigh, while Max was sleeping atop the covers on my other side with his head resting on my stomach. Both animals began to stir as they sensed my wakefulness.

I glanced out the window across the small loft from my bed. The sky was dark and the sea, which on a clear day was visible from my current vantage point, was masked in a shroud of clouds and fog. I normally don't mind the rain, but today, in anticipation of the hundreds of island residents who were bound to come out to say good-bye to one of their neighbors, I prayed the fog would lift and the rain dissipate.

Emily crawled out from under the covers and yawned as she leaned into a long stretch. I love to watch the limber kitty as she goes through her morning stretching routine. Max looked up and, noticing my wakefulness, jumped off the bed and waited patiently by the door. I put on my slippers and a warm sweatshirt, picked up Emily, and headed down the stairs. Downstairs, I let Max out through the side door, filled Emily's food and water dishes, and started a pot of coffee.

There was a chill in the air, so I lit a match and tossed it onto the wood fire Cody had kindly assembled the previous evening. I smiled as I thought about all the small things he did to take care of me that I didn't even notice while he was doing them. Not only had he anticipated my need for a fire this morning, he'd noticed I was low on milk and brought some with him when he'd come for dinner.

Max was scratching at the door to get in by the time the coffee was ready, so I dried him with a terry-cloth towel and filled his bowl with the organic food I feed him. Wet sand from the beach still clung to Max's fur, and I knew I was going to have a major sweeping job to do once he'd fully dried.

Emily followed me over to the sofa, where I curled up with a comforter and drank my coffee. My morning routine is comfortably habitual to the point of being static, even when life is hectic and unpredictable. I find that it's the small rituals that keep me grounded.

The seemingly meaningless deaths in the past few weeks had left me feeling weary. I hoped the changing tide that seemed to have brought a climate of discourse and discontent to my normally peaceful island wasn't a trend that was here to stay. Prior to the three murders in the past month, I was pretty sure Madrona Island hadn't seen a violent death in over a decade.

I took a sip of the coffee I'd laced with the milk Cody had brought and closed my eyes as the warm liquid slid down my throat and warmed me from the inside. I listened to the predicable rhythm of the waves as Emily began to purr in synchronicity. Max, who had finished his morning meal, curled up at my feet as I allowed myself a few peaceful moments before the hectic day began.

I can remember my dad telling me a long time ago that as long as you began and ended each day with a moment of quiet reflection, you would be able to deal with everything that came your way in between. I'm sure he gave me many other pieces of advice I'd promptly forgotten, but this one had stuck with me, and as often as I could, I tried to orchestrate my days accordingly.

My usual routine was to quietly drink my coffee in front of the fire on cold days or on the front deck during the summer. Once I was fully awake, I'd take Max for a run so we could both receive the fresh air and exercise we needed. I hoped if I greeted each day with a fresh perspective, I'd be able to deal with whatever challenges came my way.

At the other end of the day, as the sun set and I prepared for bed, I likewise tried to take a few minutes to sit alone with my thoughts before drifting off to sleep. Did this always work out as I intended? Not really. But I found that at times my intentions were as important as my actions.

Later that morning I joined Tara and a few hundred of our closest friends and neighbors at the cemetery on the bluff. Father Kilian was standing under an umbrella, speaking with several members of the congregation. I looked around for Cody and noticed that Maggie and her best friend, Marley, were off to the side, speaking to Sister Mary. I was certain Mr. Parsons would want to attend the service, but I wasn't sure Cody would be able to manage his wheelchair with all the mud created by the steady precipitation.

"It looks like a good turnout in spite of the weather," Tara commented.

"I wasn't expecting anything less," I said. "Mrs. Trexler was a popular woman, and only a few of us know why she was murdered. Most believe she was an innocent victim, in the wrong place at the wrong time."

"I'm glad you and Maggie arranged for the details of her death to be kept under wraps," Tara added. "It really wouldn't do anyone any good to reveal her secret at this point. I still have a hard time believing everything that's occurred in the past few weeks."

"Tell me about it," I agreed.

I looked around at the crowd gathered under the dark sky. I knew almost everyone in attendance. The steady drumming of the rain on my umbrella provided a rhythmic beat that seemed to emulate the voice of mourning.

I waved to Cody, who had shown up with Mr. Parsons as well as Maggie's next-door neighbor, Francine Rivers. The small group headed toward where Tara and I stood on the bluff overlooking the angry sea.

"I'm glad you felt up to coming out." I leaned over and kissed Mr. Parsons on the cheek. I'd noticed a glow about him since Cody had moved in and Francine had begun visiting him on a regular basis.

"A person ought to take the opportunity to pay his respects," Mr. Parsons answered. "Susan Trexler was a good woman. I'm still having a hard time believing our Ms. Winters would kill her, even if she had slipped into a state of insanity. Have you heard anything new about her situation?"

"I just know she's been admitted into a psychiatric facility and is receiving the care and evaluation she needs," I told him.

"If someone told me the island had been exposed to some sort of mind-altering gas I wouldn't even be surprised," Francine said. "First Kim kills Keith and then Ms. Winters kills Sue Trexler. We've barely had a chance to catch our breath and now someone has gone and killed poor Orson. It really is just too absurd."

I hated to say it, but I had to agree. It truly was absurd.

"Any news about Orson's murder?" Mr. Parsons asked. "I always rather liked the guy."

"No, not that I've heard," I answered.

"I've known Orson since we were kids." Mr. Parsons bowed his head. "I just can't imagine who would do such a thing. Sure, he could be boisterous and opinionated at times, but he had a good heart."

"I told you," Francine asserted. "Crazy gas. It really is the only explanation."

I smiled at the tender glance Francine shared with Mr. Parsons when they thought no one was looking. I doubted a romance was in the offing; Mr. Parsons was an old man and Francine had been single since she'd lost her husband when she was a young bride. But it seemed obvious that a genuine friendship had been established during the past couple of weeks.

"It looks like they're getting ready to start," Cody commented. "We should head over."

Tara, Francine, and I walked behind Cody, who pushed Mr. Parsons toward the open grave, where the brief service and burial would take place. Maggie and Marley had wandered over to stand with us, and Danny had shown up with a couple of the guys in the band he occasionally plays in. My mom had arrived with Cassidy, and Banjo and Summer had arrived shortly after Bella and Tansy.

The rain stopped and the clouds parted, allowing the sun to peek through as the crowd paid their last respects. I looked up at the sky and prayed that the arrival of the sun was a sign that things were going to get better, and the island would once again be the peaceful place I'd always loved.

Cody laced his fingers through mine as Father Kilian began to speak. In spite of what she had done to Maggie, I knew I'd miss visiting the retired teacher every Tuesday and Thursday afternoon, as I had for the past several years. What had started as an attempt to help out a woman who was having a difficult time getting around by bringing her food and groceries had developed into a genuine friendship.

"Do you know who brought this crab dip?" Banjo asked an hour later, after the mourners had assembled in the multipurpose room at the church.

"I'm sorry, I don't."

"It's really good. It has a kick I wasn't expecting. I'd love to get the recipe."

"Tara might know. I think she helped organize the food," I said.

"I'll be sure to ask her. Those wraps are pretty tasty as well."

I picked up a small turkey wrap and began nibbling on the corner. I wasn't really hungry, but I was antsy, and eating gave me something to do.

"Shame about Orson," Banjo commented as he scooped a large helping of potato salad onto his plate. "Guess there will be another funeral to attend in a few days."

"Maybe," I answered. "Orson's family lives on the East Coast. I imagine they may hold the funeral there."

"I guess that makes sense." Banjo picked through the selection of cheeses.

"I suppose you heard that I found the body just down the beach from your place," I whispered. "You didn't happen to see or hear anything on Sunday night, did you?"

Banjo thought about it. "I didn't hear any arguing, if that's what you're asking. I did hear the sound of a boat passing our property at around two or three a.m. I thought it was odd, because boats usually don't pass by that close to shore unless they're going to pull up onto the beach."

"Did you tell Finn this?" I asked.

"Nope. He didn't ask."

"Did you see the boat?"

"Nope. Just heard it."

"Did it sound like a large or a small boat?"

Banjo scratched his chin. "Hard to tell. I guess it sounded more like a fishing boat than a speed boat. I never owned a boat myself, so I can't say I know one from the other with any certainty. You might ask

Summer. She got up to get some water, so she might have seen something."

I looked around the room. Summer was speaking to Bella, who was standing on the far side of the room. "Okay, thanks. I think I'll wander over there and speak to her now."

Moving across a room where the occupants were packed tighter than sardines was more difficult than I had anticipated. By the time I made it to the spot near the stage where I'd seen Summer standing, she'd moved on. Bella, however, was still in the same place, chatting with Maggie.

"Caitlin, how nice to see you. I love your dress," Bella commented. The tall blonde with the waist-length hair was wearing a long black dress with fitted sleeves and buttons down the front.

"Thank you," I answered politely. "Yours is nice as well." I looked around the room. "Did you see where Summer went?"

"I believe she's chatting with Mr. Parsons," Bella answered.

I frowned.

"She doesn't have the answer you seek," Bella added. "Perhaps you should strike up a conversation with Wilbur."

"Wilbur?" Wilbur Browman was a true beach bum who made a living scavenging scraps with his metal detector and lived in a waterproof tent on the beach.

"Who better to ask about a beach landing than a man who lives on the beach?" Bella smiled.

"I guess you have a point."

"You want to find out about a beach landing?" Maggie asked.

"I'll fill you in later," I promised.

Maggie smiled in understanding.

I chatted with Maggie and Bella for a few more minutes and then dove back into the crowd to look for Wilbur. Chances were good I'd find him near the food. I realized after I walked away that I must be getting used to Bella and Tansy's witchy ways because it hadn't even occurred to me to wonder how Bella knew I was looking for information about a boat landing on the beach.

Wilbur Browman is an interesting person. He once was a very successful stock broker worth millions of dollars. He'd lived a high-profile life in a high-profile profession and enjoyed all the perks of his success, including a private jet, fast cars, and even faster women. When the economic crash sent his world shattering around him, Wilbur had liquidated what little he had left and bought a one-way ticket west, and he'd been living on the beach on Madrona Island ever since.

He spent his days surfing and looking for valuables to pawn. The simple life he lived these days wasn't my cup of tea, but it seemed to suit him; by all appearances, he seemed happy.

By the time I tracked Wilbur down he was talking to Cody about stock trends and good versus bad investments in the current day and time.

"You looking to invest?" I asked Cody as a means of entering the conversation.

"Not really. I'm putting most of my money into the newspaper, but it did occur to me that I should probably diversify a bit. Wilbur was just giving me some pointers."

Wilbur had traded his trademark cutoff jeans, tattered tank, and ratty loafers for slacks, a dress shirt, and polished shoes. He didn't even look like the same man. I was surprised to find that he was quite good-looking once he'd shaved his ratty beard and washed and trimmed his hair.

"You look nice," I complimented Wilbur.

"You hitting on me?" the man, who was a good twenty years my senior, asked.

"No, I'm just paying you a compliment to soften you up in advance of grilling you for information," I answered honestly.

Wilbur laughed. "Fair enough. What do you want to know?"

I asked about the boat Banjo had heard the night Orson's body had been dumped.

"It was foggy," Wilbur told me. "I saw the silhouette of a boat heading south close to shore. It looked like it was maybe a thirty-footer. It had a small cabin and high sides. If I had to guess I'd say it was a fishing boat, although it seemed a little early in the day for fishing."

"Banjo said he thought it was around two or three," I commented.

"Closer to two. If you're looking for the boat that delivered Orson to the beach, in my opinion the odds are better that the body was delivered by a four-wheel drive that could have driven down the beach."

I remembered that Finn had pulled up on the beach when he responded to Orson's murder, so it made sense that another similarly equipped vehicle could have driven on the beach as well. "Okay, then, do you remember hearing or seeing a vehicle in the area?"

"Nope. But I'm camped quite a ways to the north of the place where the body was found. If the vehicle came from the south I wouldn't have heard it. You might check with Grover Cloverdale. He lives to the south of the spot."

"Thanks. I'll do that. And if you can remember anything at all about the boat you saw, let me know."

"Will do, pretty lady."

I went in search of Grover Cloverdale but was told he'd already left. I knew he was going to be at the "emergency" island council meeting that night. This would be the second such meeting in as many weeks, but with everything that had occurred regarding the membership of the council, as well as the condominium development that appeared to be in a state of suspended animation due to recent events, it made sense that the members would feel it was best to convene again to figure out exactly what they were going to do.

Maggie was one of the candidates for the two open council seats and, as a candidate, had been asked to attend. The meeting promised to be a lively event I'd considered attending as well. It had been rumored that the council was about to make a decision about the hotly contested condo project that had been tearing the island apart. If that was true, there were going to be a whole lot of angry folks by the end of the day, no matter how the vote turned out.

I was looking around the room for Tara when I spotted John Goodwin, a retired fishing boat owner who now worked part-time for the Washington State ferry system. John normally worked the car deck on the ferry that served the islands, so there was a good chance he'd been on board the day Orson had arrived on the island. I changed direction and headed toward the front of the room, where he was talking to a man I didn't recognize.

"If it isn't Caitie Hart," John greeted me. John was the only person who ever called me Caitie. To clarify, John was the only person I *allowed* to call me Caitie.

"I'm fine, considering the situation." I smiled at the man John was speaking to. "I had a few questions for you, if we could speak privately when you're finished here."

"We were just wrapping up," the man informed me. "It was good talking to you. I'll see you next time I make the trip to the mainland."

John shook the man's hand before he walked away. Then he turned to look at me. "What can I do for you, Caitie girl?"

"I was wondering if you were working the island ferry on Sunday."

"Yeah, I was working. Why?"

"Did you see Orson when he arrived on the island?"

"We chatted for a minute."

"Did he mention that he had plans to meet with anyone?" I fished.

"Actually, he did," John verified. "The five-thirty ferry was a few minutes late, and Orson mentioned that he was going to be late for his six o'clock dinner appointment."

"Did he say who he was meeting?"

"No, I can't say that he did. We only spoke for a minute when he came down off the passenger deck to return to his car."

"Did he mention where he planned to have dinner?"

"Somewhere in Harthaven. The only reason I know that is because he said that once we docked he still had to drive there."

"Okay, thanks."

"You think his dinner date had something to do with his murder?" John asked.

"Honestly, I have no idea, but at this point the dinner is the only lead I have."

"You investigating again?"

"Not officially," I hedged. "In fact, I promised Finn I'd stay out of it. It's just that . . ."

"You can't let go of the idea that with a little effort you can figure it out," John supplied.

"Something like that."

Chapter 6

By the time I arrived at the council meeting, the school auditorium, where it was being held, was packed. As I suspected, half the residents of the island felt they had good reason to attend the meeting that would decide such a sensitive issue. For those of you who need to be caught up on everything that's been going on, here's a quick review. (I warn you, it can get complicated.)

A developer named Bill Powell had bought up a lot of land on the island with the intention of building affordable housing in the form of condominiums. Or at least that's what he told people. Most of the island's residents who didn't support the project, including me, thought his claim that the condos would be affordable was just a ploy to get the project approved. Most felt that once the development was completed, it would attract mainlanders looking for vacation homes, and as a result the cost of the condos would skyrocket.

Those residents who opposed the project were of the opinion that a development of this type would spoil the small town feel the island currently projects. Madrona has always enjoyed a charm devoid of large commercial businesses and real estate. There are families who have lived on the island for generations that would like to keep it that way.

Having said that, there are other longtime residents who supported the project. Those folks argued that with the change in financial status suffered by many people after fishing became regulated and the cannery closed, the only hope they had of remaining on the island was an affordable alternative to single-family homes.

From the onset, the project had been highly emotional and controversial. The *real* problem arose, however, when certain men, desperate to see the project approved, bribed and subsequently blackmailed two of the council members. This act of financial persuasion ended with the arrest of both the district bank manager and one of Bill Powell's employees. It also resulted in the early retirement of one of the council members.

To make matters worse, Cody and I discovered that a key piece of property, which gave the project water access, had been obtained illegally. The legal owner of the land had refused to sell, affectively killing the project, according to Bill Powell.

Those who would like to see the project approved were present to argue that the council should force Banjo, the individual who owns the property in question, to sell it for the common good. I'm not sure that would even be legal, but there are those citing other examples of eminent domain.

On the other side of the controversy, an equally large group have shown up to insist that due to all the illegal activities surrounding the project, there should be an immediate denial of the building application.

To add fuel to the proverbial fire, the five-person council now consists of only three people. A special election is planned, but in the meantime, two of the three remaining council members had sold land to Bill Powell, creating a conflict of interest for the council as a whole. Powell is threatening to pull out, leaving both the landowners who sold him their land at a discount in the hope of future gain, and the residents who put down large deposits on units that haven't as yet been started, up the metaphorical creek without a paddle.

It isn't an easy conflict to navigate, and in the end, there will be as many furious people on the island as happy ones, no matter what happens.

I'd hoped to speak to Grover before the meeting, but I could see there was no way I was going to get close to him until the meeting was adjourned. So I did the only thing I could—I settled in against the wall at the back of the room where I could observe the fireworks.

"This should be interesting," Cody said as he squeezed into the small space next to me.

"Interesting is putting it mildly. I'll be amazed if this doesn't end in bloodshed."

"It does seem like the crowd is ready to storm the council if things don't go their way. I'm surprised this wasn't handled behind closed doors."

"I think they intended to, but the crowd wasn't having it," I replied.

I looked to the front of the room, where the council, as well as the candidates for the open seats, had gathered. Mayor Bradley, who not only represented the council but was one of the landowners who stood to make a bundle if the project was approved, sat in the center. To his right sat Grover Cloverdale, another council member who stood to make a profit if the project went forward. To Bradley's left sat Byron Maxwell, who was firmly against the condos.

The five candidates for the council sat behind the three council members. Aunt Maggie and Francine Rivers were both against the project, while Porter Wilson and Drake Moore had come out in support of it. The fifth candidate, Rick Nesbit, had aligned himself right down the middle.

Banjo and Summer sat in the front row to the left and Bill Powell and a couple of his employees were in the front to the right. I looked around the room for Finn. I had a feeling his presence was going to be required before the night was over.

I watched as Mayor Bradley called the meeting to order. Despite my own preference, I thought both sides had legitimate opinions. Banjo was the legal owner of land that had been illegally taken from him. Now that the illegal seizure had been made public and his property had been returned to him, he had the right to sell or not as he saw fit. On the other hand, the good men and women who had forked over their hard-earned dollars as deposits on condos that would never be built were going to be out a lot of money if Bill's claim was correct and the contracts they'd signed did not require the deposits to be returned in the case of permit denial.

The only person I had zero sympathy for was Bill Powell. Although there was no proof that he had done anything illegal to this point, the man was smart and had positioned things so he came out smelling like a rose no matter the outcome.

"What do you think is going to happen?" I asked Cody.

"I don't think the council has grounds to force Banjo to sell his land, so unless he changes his mind I'm betting the project is dead."

"That would seem to be the only conclusion that makes any sense. I have a feeling it's going to be quite a while before the inevitable is actually voted on, though."

"It does seem like there are a lot of people who have petitioned to speak on both sides," Cody said.

"I spoke to John at the funeral today." I whispered. Cody and I were standing against the wall in the back of the room, so I decided to fill Cody in on my conversation as a means of passing the time. "He spoke to Orson when he arrived on the ferry. It seems he had dinner plans in Harthaven at six, but John didn't know who he was meeting. Provided Orson's dinner was in a restaurant and not at a private residence, it should be easy to find out who he met with."

"Yeah, there are only . . ." Cody paused as he performed a mental calculation, "five restaurants in Harthaven that are open on Sundays. Still, didn't Finn already tell us he put out feelers to the local restaurants?"

"It's the only lead we have," I pointed out. "What could it hurt to follow up?"

Cody shrugged.

"As far as I know, the only restaurants open on Sunday are Antonio's, Harding Pizza, the Fresh Catch, the Burger Hut, and Rosita's," I listed. "We just need to track down one employee from each location who worked on Sunday and ask if Orson came in."

"I know Orson was on a restricted diet due to his health, so I doubt he went to either Harding Pizza or the Burger Hut," Cody said.

"Maria Mendoza works at Rosita's and I saw her here earlier," I commented. "And I saw Antonio in the crowd. Why don't we split up and look for Antonio or Maria? You head to the left and I'll go to the right. We'll meet back here in fifteen minutes."

"What about the Fresh Catch?" Cody asked.

"If you see anyone who works there ask about Orson, and I'll do the same."

I set off through the crowd in one direction while Cody headed in the other. I was lucky to run into Maria almost immediately. She told me she had worked on Sunday but hadn't seen Orson. She'd been working the front desk, so she would have seen him if he'd been there. I looked around for Antonio but couldn't find him in the crowd, so I returned to the spot where I was to meet Cody."

"He didn't go to Rosita's," I said when he joined me.

"Yeah, and he wasn't at the Fresh Catch either. Did you run into Antonio?"

"No, I couldn't find him," I answered. "Let's keep our eye out for him. Given the process of elimination, it looks like that's where Orson ate."

"It's possible Orson went to someone's house for dinner," Cody speculated.

"Yeah. Maybe. But if he did, our one and only lead is dead."

Cody squeezed my hand in a show of support.

The speeches by members of the community droned on endlessly, though if I was reading the expressions of the council members correctly, it appeared they were prepared to take the path of least resistance and deny Bill Powell's building permit. I was about to sneak away and head home when a tall man took the podium. He looked familiar, but I couldn't immediately place him. I listened intently as he identified himself as an attorney representing Bill Powell. He made it clear to all who were present that the land obtained by Powell Development from longstanding members of the island community, including Mayor Bradley's wife and Grover Coverdale, had been purchased legally at the agreed upon price, and no additional compensation would be offered if the condominium project wasn't approved.

I could see the shift in energy as the people who had sold their land to Powell began to consider the amount of money they stood to lose if they denied the permit. But they were in a tight spot, with Powell continuing to insist that the project was dead without the land owned by Banjo. Banjo and Summer seemed equally intent on hanging on to what they had.

There was a brief discussion among the council members that centered on finding a legal way of forcing Banjo to sell his land, but those in the room who opposed the project tossed out conflict-of-interest accusations, and the discussion died.

"Well, that was a waste," I said to Emily when I got home. "Not only am I no closer to knowing where Orson ate on Sunday night but I had to listen to what seemed like endless arguments about the condo project."

"Meow."

"I know what you mean. Watching the community I love self-destruct before my very eyes isn't an easy thing to do. I hate to say this, but I'm concerned that relationships that have existed for generations may dissolve in the face of such a financially volatile controversy. It seems to me that Powell set things up just a little too neatly. It almost feels like he'd be better off if the project does turn out to be a bust. He certainly won't suffer."

"Meow, meow."

"No, I never did have a chance to talk to Grover and, no, I didn't figure out who Orson had dinner with on Sunday night, which means I'm no closer to finding Orson's killer than I was before I subjected myself to all that mind-numbing arguing."

"Meow."

"Yeah, I've begun to think that as well."

I cuddled the kitten to my chest. She was turning out to be a pretty good conversationalist. Not that I spoke cat. Still, what I feel certain Emily was pointing out was that Bella, who knows everything, had directed me toward Wilbur. If I was really meant to get information from Grover or Orson's dining partner, why wouldn't Bella simply send me in that direction in the first place? If I had realized that sooner I could have stayed home and spared myself the scene of an island family disintegrating before my very eyes.

"So the question is," I lifted my feline friend so we were eye to eye, "was Wilbur lying about what he knows or does he just not yet realize he knows something?"

"Meow." Emily swatted at my nose.

"Yeah, I was thinking that too. Chances are Wilbur knows something he hasn't yet comprehended he knows. I guess we should go see him again."

Emily wriggled down and trotted over to the door.

"Not now, you silly cat. It's late. I'll go tomorrow."

I swear Emily would have shrugged if cats could shrug. She jumped up onto the kitchen counter and began chasing a pen back and forth across the smooth surface. Max looked up to check out what exactly was making the rolling sound before yawning and going back to sleep.

It was a pleasant evening. I'd opened the windows to allow the sound of the surf to flow naturally into my tiny kingdom. It wasn't quite cold enough for a fire, but I built a small one anyway to provide atmosphere, then lit a couple of scented candles, poured a glass of wine, and wrapped myself in an afghan. Max slept on the sofa next to me while Emily continued to play with the pen. It was a perfect moment, and for the first time all day I felt myself relax.

I let the sound of the waves lull me into a relaxed state as I tried to figure out what it was Wilbur might know. I didn't get the sense that he was lying to me or intentionally keeping a secret, so if I was to discover whatever it was Bella seemed to think I should, I needed to figure out the right question to ask to unlock Wilbur's memory.

Emily must have tired of her game because she jumped off the counter and began to run around the room from one piece of furniture to the next. She certainly was wound up, but then again, I'd been gone for most of the day, so she must have already slept quite a bit. I watched the hyper kitten as she ran across the room, executed a complete midair turn, and then pounced on something only she could see.

"Something only she could see," I whispered to myself.

Wilbur admitted to having seen the boat. It was dark and foggy, so he couldn't make out any details, but what if he had seen more than he remembered? I'd already realized it was up to me to unlock his deepest memories. I suddenly wondered if they had *The Idiot's Guide to Hypnotism* online.

Chapter 7

Thursday, June 11

I woke to find Emily staring me in the face. A quick glance out the window confirmed that the sun hadn't as of yet begun its ascent. My inclination was to roll over and go back to sleep. The problem was that when I tried to do just that, the silly kitten climbed up onto the dresser, then used the height provided to pounce onto my head.

"Cut it out," I said, swatting at the playful feline. "I have another hour before I need to get up."

Emily burrowed under the covers and began biting my toes. Clearly I was going to need to come to grips with the fact that the kitten wanted her breakfast and was unwilling to wait another hour to get the attention she felt she deserved. I groaned as I flung back the covers. I sat up and slid my legs over the side of the bed. Maybe if I got up early enough I could take Max for a quick run before I headed into town to meet Tara for exercise class.

"Okay, I'm up." I yawned as I slipped my feet into a pair of slippers and pulled my knee-length hoodie over the boxers and tank I wore to sleep in. I stumbled down the stairs in the dark and opened the door so that Max could go out. I continued on into the kitchen and turned on the coffeepot before retrieving the kitten food from the cupboard. Once I'd provided Emily with the food and water she seemed to be impatient to receive, I went to the door to let Max back in so that he could eat his own breakfast.

It really was going to be a beautiful sunrise. It had stormed during the night, with an orchestra of rain and wind, and the last of the clouds, the majority of which had since moved on, had painted the morning sky with wispy swirls that looked as though someone had taken a thin brush and added them by hand. I pulled on a warm pair of sweatpants, poured a cup of hot coffee, and headed out onto the deck to watch as the sun turned the clouds from gray to pink to red.

The tide was out, exposing a wide stretch of sand that was underwater most of the day. I slipped off my sandals and walked out onto the wet beach. The water was cold, but the hot coffee warmed me from the inside as I sipped the liquid adrenaline. The beach was deserted in both directions as far as the eye could see. I felt at one with the universe as I watched the sun slowly peek over the horizon and rise into the sky. One of the most awesome things about my little slice of the world was that during the longest days of the year I was able to watch the sun rise and set from the beach outside my cabin.

I thought of Banjo and Summer. I knew the meeting last night had to have been hard on them. Banjo had every right to do what he wanted with the land he owned, but there were a whole lot of people who were trying to make him out to be the bad guy. If I'd been in the same situation as the peace-loving couple I'd be a total wreck, but knowing how easygoing they were I imagined they were on their own beach performing sets of salutations as the sun greeted the day.

It must be nice to approach life in such a carefree manner. In the time I'd known them I'd rarely seen them fazed by anything. Maybe one of these days I'd wander down the beach in time to join them for their morning ritual.

I walked up to the point where the gentle waves rolled onto the beach and paused before receding. A pair of bald eagles circled overhead, hunting for an early morning meal, while flocks of seagulls squawked loudly as they fought over tidbits of discarded food and dead fish they found in the sand and among the exposed rocks.

I strolled slowly down the beach with Max, who had wandered out through the open door, prancing along beside me. My bare toes were beginning to feel the effect of the cold, so I turned to head back to the cabin. Another cup of coffee, a fried egg or two, and maybe some toast. It sounded like the perfect way to start what I anticipated would be another perfect day. I hadn't been able to track down Wilbur the previous day, so chatting with him about his hidden memories was number one on my to-do list for today. After Bitzy's exercise class, of course.

I was almost back to the cabin when Max trotted up with something in his mouth. I bent over to accept the wet and slobbery gift he was so proudly offering. It appeared he'd found a hat that most likely had blown off a boat.

I tossed the hat onto the front deck of the cabin, intending to dispose of it later. I went inside and poured a second cup of coffee and then headed into the bathroom to take a shower. In a way it seemed silly to shower *before* the class that always left me in need of a shower, but I was sandy from my walk and the hot water would help to chase the last of the chill from my bones.

"Kill me now," Tara groaned as Bitzy led us through a grueling abdominal routine. Even I, the girl who liked to exercise, thought this particular routine was better suited for boot camp.

"She does seem to want to make certain she inflicts pain today," I whispered back.

"I heard her husband left her." Tara gave up and lay flat on her mat. Luckily, we were in the back of the room, so the rest of the class, who were all dealing with their own misery, weren't paying any attention to us.

"Really?" I asked as I lifted my shoulders for what had to be my hundredth sit-up.

"That's the rumor." Tara lifted her head and pretended to be doing a crunch, although her head was the only part of her body that left the mat. "I had lunch at the food truck that's been parking at the end of the wharf yesterday, and a couple of the women who take classes from her were discussing the fact that Bitzy's husband quit his job and left the island with the new kindergarten teacher."

"Yikes." I frowned as Bitzy continued to bark commands. The morning routine really was becoming ridiculous. I was about to join Tara in her impression of a corpse when Bitzy finally called for a cooldown. "I know Bitzy can be mean, but I kinda feel sorry for her."

"Yeah. I'm sure it isn't an easy situation to deal with," Tara agreed. "Maybe we should invite her to brunch."

"Oh God no," I countered. "I said I felt sorry for her; I didn't say I wanted to share a meal with the woman. You do remember what happened the last time we asked her to join us?"

Not only had Bitzy sent her food back three times due to some sort of problem only she seemed to be aware of but she'd criticized the choices Tara and I had made and then proceeded to explain in detail how our very delicious but less than superhealthy meals would cause us to not only suffer an early death but every kind of physical deformity imaginable along the way.

"Yeah, I guess that might not be the best idea," Tara agreed. "Besides, the painter is coming today, so I really should skip brunch and head right over to Coffee Cat Books. It's nice that you've been around the past few days."

"And I'll be around again today," I promised. "I just need to go home to shower, pick up Haley, and check in with Maggie before I head over. Oh, and talk to Wilbur. I never did track him down yesterday. I should still get to the cannery in a couple of hours or so. Do you want me to pick up something for us to eat on my way in?"

"Yeah. Maybe a salad. There's no way I want to do anything that will negate the ten thousand calories I just burned up. I'm less than five pounds away from fitting into that red dress I bought but could never wear."

"Wow. Congrats," I said as I got up off the floor and picked up my mat. I offered Tara my hand and pulled her to a standing position as well, now that Bitzy had decided she'd inflicted enough pain for one day. "Are you going to wear it to your cousin's wedding?"

"Hopefully. The wedding is still several weeks away, so I should be able to lose enough weight for it to fit by then."

"And are you bringing Carl?" I asked as we headed toward the locker room. Carl Prescott was an electrician Tara had met during the remodel of the old cannery.

"I don't know. I like Carl, and we have fun together, but introducing him to my family seems like a big step I'm not sure I'm ready for. And I don't want to send the wrong message. I sort of get the vibe that he's already a lot more serious about me than I am about him."

"Then you definitely shouldn't invite him. Is your mom still planning to come for a visit before the wedding?"

Tara had shared during last week's exercise class that her mother and aunt were planning to come to the island sooner rather than later.

"I don't know. I told her how busy I was and tried to convey how much a visit right now would be pointless because I don't have the time to spend with her that I'm certain she'll insist on, but I'm not sure I managed to change her mind. She basically said she'd think about it and let me know."

"It's too bad you don't get along with your mother better," I commented as I packed my gym bag.

"It's not that I don't get along with her; it's more that we're so different. We have virtually nothing in common. The entire time I was growing up I was certain I'd been switched at birth. I don't even look like either of my parents."

I laughed. "I doubt you were switched at birth, but I do agree you don't resemble your parents physically. Of course Siobhan and I look nothing alike and we're sisters."

"Yeah," Tara slung the strap of her gym bag over her shoulder and started toward the exit, "but you favor your mom and Siobhan looks a lot like your dad. I don't look like any of the people I'm related to."

After heading home to shower I picked up my bike and started down the beach to the place where I knew Wilbur had set up camp. I checked his tent first, but he wasn't inside, so I decided to leave my bike there and walk down the beach. He was probably either scavenging or in town visiting his regulars, who tended to invite him in for a cup of coffee or a quick snack. Although I found Wilbur's choices in life odd, he did have a pleasant way about him that most people seemed to enjoy. I supposed the handouts he received from those he stopped to chat with allowed him to live the life he chose in relative comfort.

Luckily, I found him sitting on a rock under a tree five minutes into my search. I headed toward him with a purposeful stride.

"Why is it I get the feeling this isn't a social call?" Wilbur's eyes twinkled as I approached.

"I guess because it's not. I wanted to talk to you some more about the boat you saw."

"I'm pretty sure I told you everything I know."

"Maybe." I sat down on the sand next to where he was sitting. "It's just that Bella sent me to you in the first place."

"Ah. So you figure I'm lying about what I know?"

"No. Not lying," I clarified. "I just think I might be able to help you jar your memory if you're willing to play along."

Wilbur looked at me for a moment without replying. Then he shrugged, indicating he was willing to give it a shot.

"Great. Get comfortable and close your eyes."

He winked at me, as if to insinuate that I had lewd intentions toward him, but I ignored his gesture and eventually he did as I asked. The man was certainly a flirt, although he seemed harmless enough.

"Now, I want you to remember that night. Let your mind be transported to that place in time and space."

Wilbur sat quietly. I couldn't really know what he was focusing on, so I had to assume he was doing as I asked. I continued in a gentle voice, as the how-to video I'd found on the Internet had suggested.

"You see the boat through the fog. It's dark, and all you can make out is a silhouette. It's passing close to the shore and you notice the boat has a cabin. Is the cabin tall enough to stand under?"

"Yes. It's tall enough to stand under," Wilbur answered in a robotic voice.

Now I was sure he was messing with me. There was no way he was actually in a trance, but I continued anyway.

"Is there anything distinctive about the boat? Does it have lights or a visible wench system?"

"Lights. Spotlights, to be exact. They weren't on, but I could see the silhouette of spotlights on top of the cabin," Wilbur shared.

"Great. That's good. Keep focusing on the boat."

I wasn't sure we were getting anywhere—virtually every fishing or tour boat had spotlights—but I'd take what I could get.

"Do you see any people onboard?" I asked.

Wilbur scrunched up his face. "No. I don't see any people. It's too dark to make out forms within the cabin, though."

"Okay. Can you see anything else, like fishing poles or outriggers?"

Wilbur thought about it. "No. I don't see anything like that. Now that I think about it, I don't think it's a fishing boat. Maybe a whale-watch boat?"

"Okay, we're narrowing it down. Do you see anything at all that might identify it? Maybe something unique to the shape?" I asked.

Wilbur shook his head. "Sorry. It was just too dark. I only glimpsed the boat as it passed. I heard the motor, which was what woke me up. I saw a flash through the tent walls, which made me look. And when I did look I just saw an image."

"A flash? What kind of flash?"

Wilbur thought again. "I don't know. A flash of light. Maybe whoever was in the boat turned on the spotlight for a minute and then turned it back off. Although the flash seemed to be red." Wilbur opened his eyes. "I guess if you can find a boat with a red spotlight you'll have your boat."

I thanked Wilbur, went back to the tent to pick up my bike, and continued on toward town. If he'd seen a red flash of light what he'd seen was probably the sheriff's boat. I'd have to ask Finn if the boat had been out that night. But why would a member of the sheriff's department have been out cruising around without his lights on?

By the time I got to the old cannery, which was looking more and more like a bookstore these days, Tara was suited up with her hardhat and clipboard and the dozen or so men who were working that day were already busily engaged in activity. I slipped a hardhat onto my head and wandered over to where she was talking to one of the subcontractors. Once the place was painted the floor would be installed, and then we'd be able to begin building shelves, cabinets, and other interior adornments. The inventory Tara had ordered was scheduled to be delivered right after the Fourth of July weekend. Tara seemed certain we'd be able to open in August, and now that I could see how fast things were moving along, I felt certain she'd meet her goal.

"How can I help?" I asked after Tara finished her conversation.

"Did you bring lunch?"

"No," I said, hanging my head. "I forgot."

"Now that my muscles have stopped screaming I'm really hungry. The food truck is fine if you don't mind running over and picking something up."

"I'm on my way. Anything special you'd like?"

"Surprise me."

The truck was parked at the end of the wharf, near where the ferry docked. The boat had just recently unloaded its passengers, so the line at the portable eatery was longer than I would have preferred. But it would take me even longer to go for something to take out, so I took my place behind a group of tourists who had probably come to the island for a long weekend. I have to say I share the love/hate relationship with our visitors that many other locals do. On one hand, most of the residents wouldn't be able to live here at all if it weren't for the income they bring to the island, but on the other, our normally deserted beaches and hiking trials become overrun with day trippers and weekend travelers who come to the island to enjoy our mild temperatures and spotless beaches.

"Is that little Caitlin Hart?" I heard a voice say from behind me.

I cringed as I turned around. "Valerie. What brings you to Pelican Bay?"

"I heard Cody West was on the island."

Valerie and Cody had dated for almost a year during high school.

"I don't suppose you know where I might find him?" Val asked. "I called the number I had for him, but it was disconnected."

"I imagine he's changed it at least once in the past ten years," I commented.

"Yes, I suppose so. I figured when I couldn't get hold of him by phone I'd just toodle out to the island and say hi. Do you know where I can find him?" the blond-haired Barbie doll asked.

Seeing Val brought back old jealousies that made me want to pull out her hair by its platinum roots, but Cody might actually want to see her, so I decided to tell her the truth.

"Cody bought the old newspaper. He's been working to fix up the office, so I'd imagine that's where you'll find him."

Valerie frowned, marring her perfectly applied makeup. "He bought the old newspaper? Whatever for?"

"I guess he thought owning a newspaper would be rewarding. You do remember he was on the school paper?"

"Well, sure, but I was a cheerleader and it's not like I went on to get a job as a Laker Girl. I thought Cody was some sort of spy or something."

I looked away to keep from laughing. Spy? "Cody was in the Navy," I explained. "Technically, I guess he still is, but he has plans to retire and run the paper."

"Well, that's disappointing." Val tapped one of the toes of her bright pink shoes. "I did come all this way, though, so I guess I should at least drop by to say hi." She looked down at her five-inch heels. "I don't suppose you have your car nearby? I could really use a ride."

"I'm sorry; I rode my bike into town."

"I see. Well, I guess I'll have to find a taxi."

"On Madrona Island?" I asked.

"They still don't have a taxi service on this godforsaken island?"

"'Fraid not."

"I have a truck nearby," a man standing in line behind me offered.

Val looked him up and down. I could tell she was assessing his appearance. God forbid that she be seen with anyone who might be wearing work clothes. The man had on a pair of slacks and a polo shirt. I didn't recognize him, so I assumed he was a visitor who had brought his vehicle over on an earlier ferry.

"Yes, well, I guess that would be okay." Val looked down at her white miniskirt. "Your truck is clean, isn't it?"

"I just had it detailed on Tuesday," the man answered.

"Well, okay, then." Val turned to look at me. "It was nice talking to you."

I watched as Val looped her arm thorough her temporary chauffeur's and walked away in her high heels. Val was Cody's age, so she was two years older than me, and while we were never close, we did tend to run in similar circles during her time at Madrona High School because she'd dated both Cody and Danny. I thought about calling Cody and warning him that Val was on her way, but why ruin the surprise? He'd probably be thrilled to see the ridiculous woman.

Chapter 8

By the time Tara and I had finished at Coffee Cat Books for the day I was exhausted. What I really wanted to do was go home, pull on some sweats, and take a long, slow walk on the beach, but I'd been thinking about Cody and Valerie all day, and the childish part of me that I feared would never grow up really wanted to see if the pair were still together. Val hadn't had any luggage with her, but that didn't mean she wouldn't stay given half a chance. I tried to tell myself that I didn't care who Cody did or did not spend time with, but even I knew I was lying to myself.

I called Cody with the pretense of finding out if he had anything new to share about Orson's death, but he didn't answer. What I should have done at that point was go home, take Max for a walk, play with Emily, and get to bed early. What I did was set out on my bike to find Cody. Although it was after six, the sun was still high in the sky, so I had plenty of time to track him down before it got dark.

I stopped at the newspaper office, but he wasn't there. I called Mr. Parsons, who informed me that he hadn't seen Cody all day, but that Francine was at the house with him to share a meal and watch a movie. I headed back down Main Street and peeked in through the window of the few restaurants the town provided. Madrona Island wasn't all that big; if he wasn't in Pelican Bay he was most likely in Harthaven. I knew I didn't have time to ride my bike to Harthaven, so I headed home with half an idea to pick up my ancient car and head toward the fishing village to the north.

When I arrived at my small cabin Cody was sitting on the front deck.

"What are you doing here?" I asked as I leaned my bike against the wall of the cabin.

"Waiting for you. You're late."

"I had some errands," I lied. "I tried to call you, but you didn't pick up."

Cody frowned and looked at his phone. "I do have a missed call from you. I didn't hear it ring. Why didn't you leave a message?"

I shrugged. "It wasn't important. So did Val find you?" I asked.

"Unfortunately, yes. She hasn't changed a bit."

"I know you dated," I said casually. "I thought you might be happy to see her."

"I enjoyed dating a sixteen-year-old girl when I was sixteen, but I have absolutely no interest in spending time with a twenty-eight year old who acts like a sixteen year old now that I'm twenty-eight. The hour we spent together was excruciating."

I smiled.

"Have you had dinner?" Cody asked.

"No, not yet."

"Do you want to head into town to grab something?"

"I'd love to, but I need to let Max out, feed Emily, and then see to the cats in the sanctuary. Maggie is having dinner with Marley this evening, so I told her I'd take care of the cats."

"I'll help you and then we can get a bite. I'm dying for some fresh seafood."

"Okay." I opened my front door and headed inside. Max greeted me with the happy dog dance. He wasn't used to me being away for such long periods of time, but with all the construction going on I hated to bring him into town with me when I planned to spend the day at Coffee Cat Books.

"Why don't you take Max for a walk while I see to Emily and the cats in the sanctuary?" I suggested.

"Okay. Come on, Max. Let's spend some of that pent-up energy of yours."

I watched Cody as he jogged down the beach with Max running happily beside him. The sun was just beginning its descent in the distance, and the image of the man and dog framed by the setting sun was something worth capturing. I pulled out my phone and snapped a quick photo.

I then headed over to the cat sanctuary, which is really Maggie's baby. After some of the feral cats that populate the island got into Mayor Bradley's pond and killed some of his expensive koi, he'd sponsored a law that made it legal to remove cats from your property by any means available. While many of the island's residents rounded up the cats and dropped them at shelters on the mainland, others chose to make a sport of hunting the cats and eliminating them permanently.

Maggie had opened the sanctuary in the hope that the island residents would take a humane approach if presented with one. Thankfully, most did. The adult feral cats were trapped and altered. Those that were able to be domesticated were eventually adopted into forever families, while those that were unable to make the transition were given permanent asylum in the sanctuary, which provided both indoor rooms and completely covered outdoor runs. Any kittens born there or brought to the facility at a young age were socialized, altered, and given shots before Maggie and I sought forever homes for our "kids."

"Evening, Moose," I said. He was one of the first cats trapped, but he was much too grouchy to be placed in a forever home. He seemed to like me okay, and he let Maggie pet him when he was in the mood, but he absolutely adored Haley.

I picked up the huge orange tabby and scratched him behind the ear for the ten seconds he let me before struggling to get down. I cleaned his cat box, filled his food and water bowls, and shook out his bed. Moose liked to sit up high, so we'd built him a kitty tower. Now he could climb up there and survey his kingdom from afar, and it was from atop this perch that he watched as I worked.

I moved on to the other lifetime residents before making my way to the nursery, where moms with kittens were kept in separate enclosures. Haley spent hours every day playing with the kittens once they were old enough for it. I could see a difference in the socialization of the kittens, as well as several of the mothers, since she'd been assisting us.

Cody joined me in the toddler room, which we used for weaned kittens that hadn't been placed in homes yet. "Max is exercised and fed."

"Thanks," I replied. "I'm almost done."

Cody pitched in to refill food and water dishes.

"Have you talked to Finn today?" Cody asked.

"Only for a minute. I did manage to talk to Wilbur. He remembered seeing a flash of red light from the boat he saw on the night Orson died. I asked Finn, and he said the sheriff's boat wasn't out that night. Can you think of any other boats in the area that have a cabin and are around thirty feet long that might have a red spotlight?"

"Not offhand," Cody answered. "I'll keep my eyes open, though."

"I thought I'd ask Danny. He's pretty familiar with all the boats in the area."

"Are you sure Wilbur didn't just see the port light?" Cody asked.

"No, he said it was bright. More like a spotlight, but it was only on for a moment. By the time he got up and looked out of his tent the boat was dark."

I set the kitten I'd been holding on the ground, and it immediately bounded over to Cody and began to climb up his pants leg. There was one thing for sure: this little guy wasn't shy or scared of humans. We really needed to find him a home. Maybe I'd take him with me to the adoption clinic I planned to attend next Saturday. It would be awesome once Coffee Cat Books opened. I hoped we'd be able to find homes for our charges through the cat room so I wouldn't need to make the trip to the mainland quite so often.

"Have you read the entire journal Orson left?" I asked. I hoped there would be additional clues in it.

"Yeah. It was really just a bunch of notes about his research into Maryellen Thornton's disappearance, as well as notes and impressions from his conversations with Jane Farmington. He seemed pretty convinced they were one and the same."

"Were there photos of either Maryellen or Jane in his files?" I wondered as I began locking up the sanctuary.

"Not in his notes, but I'm sure we can find photos of Maryellen online. The murder of her family and her disappearance were national news."

"I'm starving right now. Let's go eat, and then we can come back here to see what we can find."

After dinner I poured us both glasses of wine while Cody logged onto my computer. We decided to work at the kitchen table, which provided a scenic backdrop as well as adequate light with which to make notes. It felt domestically cozy to settle in with Cody at the end of a long day. Emily jumped onto the table and began to purr louder than I've ever heard a kitten purr when Cody pulled up the information on Maryellen Thornton.

"It looks like Maryellen was only ten at the time of her disappearance," Cody informed me. "There are quite a few photos of Mr. and Mrs. Thornton that made the media rounds at the time, but so far I haven't found any of Maryellen."

"Maybe her parents were careful to protect her from the probing eyes of the press when they were alive," I speculated.

"I guess that makes sense," Cody agreed. "She was the heiress to a fortune, so I'm sure her parents wanted to keep her off the radar of anyone who might want to kidnap her for a ransom."

"I've been thinking about that. If Orson was correct and she was seen alive ten years after her parents were killed, she must have been kidnapped. I wonder why the kidnapper didn't ask for a ransom."

"If Maryellen was kidnapped, and we don't know that for certain," Cody reminded me, "and whoever did it intended to ask for money, we have to assume the kidnapper didn't mean to kill her parents. It makes sense that her other relatives wouldn't have been quite as motivated to get her back safely. I mean, look at how quickly they had her declared legally dead."

"That's true. If the kidnapper didn't intend to kill the Thorntons I wonder what happened."

"We'll most likely never know."

Cody continued to search while I rummaged around in the refrigerator for a snack. Our dinner had been delicious, but for some reason it hadn't really stuck with me, and I found I was still hungry. I put together a plate with cheese, crackers, and fruit and set it on the table.

"I found something," Cody said as I sat down after returning to the refrigerator to retrieve the wine bottle. "It's a photo of Maryellen with her parents at a fund-raiser when she was eight."

I leaned over Cody's shoulder and looked at the photo, which showed a tall, thin man dressed in a suit standing next to a tall, thin woman dressed in a straight black dress. Standing next to the woman was a small girl with dark hair. No one in the photo was smiling. It appeared almost as if they were wax figures that had been posed just so.

"They don't look like they were having any fun," I commented. "Does that little girl look familiar to you?"

"Yeah, I guess her features do seem familiar. I'm sure we must have seen other photos of her somewhere. Her disappearance was a huge deal when it happened, even though we weren't even born yet. Still, I'd be willing to bet the murder and kidnapping has been talked about on the news since then, even if we're having a hard time finding photos of Maryellen now."

"Maybe." Somehow I had a feeling it was more than that.

Cody reached for a piece of cheese just as Emily leaped onto the computer keyboard.

"Whoa, little lady." Cody picked up the playful kitten. "What was that all about?"

"Maybe she thinks you need to watch your weight," I joked.

Cody frowned.

"I'm just kidding. Your weight is fine."

Cody continued to stare at the screen.

"You're such a girl. One little comment about your weight and you're giving me the silent treatment."

"It's not that. Look what popped up on the screen when Emily jumped on the keyboard."

I looked over Cody's shoulder again. There was a photo of a crowd of people standing on the passenger deck of one of the ferries that served the San Juan Islands. Toward the back of the crowd, standing alone and away from the crowd, was a man and a young woman who looked to be no older than twenty.

"Do you think that's them?" I asked.

"I don't know," Cody admitted. "But the woman looks like she could be Maryellen. She has similar features to the girl in the photo we just found, although her hair is blond here and Maryellen was dark in the other photo."

"I suppose that if this is Maryellen she could have bleached her hair as part of a disguise." I continued to study the photo. It really was hard to tell if this young woman with blond hair was the same person who'd been photographed next to her mother as a child. Still, she did look familiar. Really familiar. I just couldn't place where I'd seen her before. I studied her face and tried to imagine her with dark hair. The woman on the ferry deck was standing next to a man she appeared to be traveling with, but she had her shoulder turned slightly so she wasn't looking at him. Her expression was blank, like the body she possessed was merely a shell, without a consciousness or soul. She seemed to be staring into the distance.

"She sure looks like a person who's given up all hope," I commented. "If that *is* Maryellen, I wonder if the man who fathered her child was the same person who murdered her parents and kidnapped her."

"I guess stranger things have happened."

"I keep thinking I've seen her before."

"Yeah. I have the same feeling." Cody nodded.

"You don't think she stayed in the area after her husband died?"

"I don't know why she would. Still, I do feel like I've met her. She'd be quite a bit older now."

I quickly did the math. Maryellen was kidnapped in 1979. She was ten at the time, which would make her forty-six now. I tried to imagine someone who was around this age who looked like the girl in the photo, but I was coming up blank. I just knew I was going to be awake all night, trying to figure out where I'd seen the mysterious woman before. When I finally figured it out at three a.m. I wondered if I could possibly be right.

Chapter 9

Friday, June 12

In the light of day I decided the revelation I'd experienced in the middle of the night had to be nothing more than an illusion brought about by sleep deprivation. There was really no way the person I believed looked like Maryellen could possibly *be* Maryellen. There was one way to find out for certain, though, and that was to ask the person in question. I was pondering the implications of doing just that when I received a call from Haley. During the night, while I was trying to solve a puzzle that very well might not be solvable, her mother had died.

I knew Haley's mom had been sick for a long time, but I was certain that wouldn't make things any easier for the twelve year old. Her aunt was making plans for the two of them to make the trip home, and Haley wanted to be sure she had the chance to say good-bye to Maggie and me before they left. I promised Haley that I'd pick her up within the hour and called Maggie, who offered to make breakfast for the three of us.

Haley jogged up to my car and into my waiting arms as soon as I pulled up to her aunt's house. I hugged the girl who had come to mean so much to both Maggie and me in just a few short weeks.

"I'm so sorry about your mom."

Haley hugged me as hard as her young arms could squeeze. She didn't say anything at first, so I just continued to hug her, letting her set the pace. After what seemed like an eternity but was probably only a minute, she whispered, "Mom has been sick for a long time. I can barely remember a time when she hasn't been sick. Delilah says that it's for the best, that she's finally at peace and free from suffering."

"And you?" I asked. "How do you feel?"

Haley pulled away and looked at me. Her eyes were swollen, and it was obvious she'd been crying. "I know Delilah is right, but I wish I'd had the chance to tell her that I loved her."

"I'm sure she knew." I desperately sought words that would lessen the girl's grief, although deep down I knew there was nothing I could say that would be perfect enough for such an impossible task.

A single tear slid down Haley's cheek. "The thing is, I don't think she did know how I felt." Haley took several short breaths as she fought her emotions.

"Moms know these things," I assured her.

"Maybe." Tears continued to stream down her cheeks.

"Is it something else?" I instinctively asked.

Haley looked away. Her face was a kaleidoscope of emotions as she struggled to speak.

"It's natural to be sad," I offered.

Haley looked at me. "It's not that."

"Then what?" I used my thumb to wipe away her tears.

"I'm a bad person and a horrible daughter," Haley sobbed.

I held the girl as she cried. "You aren't a bad person," I insisted. "You're a wonderful person. One of the very best people I know."

"No," the girl cried. "I'm not."

I pulled back and looked her in the eye. "Why would you say that?"

"Because." Haley wiped her face with her arm.

"Because why?" I encouraged.

Haley stared into the distance. I could see she was deciding whether to confide in me.

"You can talk to me if you want to," I offered. "I won't judge. I promise."

Haley turned and looked at me. "When Del told me this morning that Mom had died and she was going to take me home now instead of in September, the very first thing I felt was anger."

"I think it's natural to feel angry when someone you love dies."

"But that's just it," Haley cried. "I wasn't angry because my mom died; I was angry because I had to go home early. My mom is dead and my first thought was that I would have to leave you and Maggie and the cats and go home to my dark, depressing life. How horrible am I?"

"You aren't horrible."

"Yes, I am." Haley began to sob even harder.

I really didn't know what to say. I understood why Haley felt bad, but I also realized she'd had a difficult time of it, and it was natural to feel sorrow at the loss of two months of living in the light only to return to the darkness. I called Maggie to tell her we would be a little late, and then I took Haley's hand

and walked her down the beach. We were silent, each lost in our own thoughts, as I prayed for the words to heal Haley's broken heart.

"My dad died a few years ago," I finally said.

"He did? I'm sorry."

"He wasn't sick the way your mom was. He died because of an accident. But in the years before he died he'd slipped into a sort of depression, and depression is a kind of sickness."

Haley didn't say anything, but I could tell I had her attention.

"When I first heard that he had died, in those very first moments before I had time to think about things," I continued, "I found that I was almost glad."

"Glad? Really? Why?" Haley stopped walking and turned to look at me.

"I guess it was because my dad had been sad for so long, and it made everyone around him sad. He was grumpy and short-tempered with those he loved, and the house I grew up in seemed to be shadowed with a darkness I didn't know how to deal with." I looked directly at Haley. "Of course once I thought about things I realized I wasn't glad my dad was dead. I knew I loved him and would miss him, and that made me feel bad for being glad he was gone, even if it was only for a minute."

"What did you do?" Haley breathed.

"I took a long walk and thought about all the wonderful things I remembered about my dad before he got so sad. The way he used to put me on his wide shoulders when I was young, and the way he smiled and scooped me into his arms when he came home from a fishing trip. I remembered how he taught me to ride a bike even though my mom thought I was too young, and I remembered the way he smelled."

"Smelled?"

"He was a fisherman and he worked really hard, so he usually smelled of salt and sweat."

"My mom used to bake cookies before she got sick," Haley shared. "She smelled like cinnamon." She smiled. "And she had this silly apron she wore when she cooked. It had a cat in a chef's hat on the front. And she used to laugh a lot. Before."

"She sounds wonderful."

"She was," Haley said. "We had a flower garden in our yard and Mom used to let me help her pick fresh flowers for the dinner table. And we liked to take long walks down by the lake. And every night when she tucked me into bed she'd braid my hair and read me a story." Haley began to cry. "I feel so bad that I'd forgotten all that."

I took Haley's hand in mine and began to walk along the water's edge again. "My mom once told me that there are two kinds of death, the kind that takes your soul and the kind that takes your spirit. My dad's spirit was taken away long before his soul was taken in death. I think I'd gotten used to the dad I loved being gone long before he left this earth. I'd already mourned the loss of that wonderful man, so when he died it didn't seem like anything had really changed. At least not at first."

"I get that," Haley commented. "The mom who baked cookies and read to me has been gone for a very long time."

"I think you and I both need to give ourselves a break," I said. "Maybe we didn't react to the news that our parent died the way we wanted to, or the way most people think we should have, but that doesn't mean I didn't love my dad and you didn't love your mom. After I thought about it for a bit I decided to write down every single wonderful thing I could remember about my dad so I would never forget the way he was before he got sad."

"You think I should do that? Write down all the stuff I can remember about my mom before she got sick?"

"I think that's up to you, but I know that when I read what I wrote it brings me comfort."

"Thanks, Cait. I'll do that."

"Are you ready to go have breakfast with Maggie?"

"And the cats?"

"And the cats."

"Poor Haley," Tara said several hours later.

"Yeah. I felt so helpless. I can understand why she would rather stay here than go back to a home that's been such a dark, depressing place for so long. Maggie is going to talk to her aunt to see if she thinks Haley's dad would allow her to come back to stay with her after the funeral."

"I'm sure that would be good for Haley, but her dad might need her to be close by."

"Yeah, that's what I thought," I agreed. "Still, maybe he would welcome the opportunity to have her cared for while he deals with his own grief."

Tara set down her clipboard and hugged me. One of the best things about her is that she always knows when I need a special Tara hug. I hugged her back, letting her warmth chase away the stress I'd been feeling since I'd spoken to Haley. Delilah planned to pick Haley up from Maggie's, so I knew I wouldn't see her again unless her dad agreed to let her spend the rest of the summer on Madrona Island.

I gave Tara one final squeeze and then took a step back, wiping the tears from my face. "I've been thinking about the paint we plan to use for the walls in the cat room," I said, changing the subject to something I had at least some control over.

"What about it?" Tara took my cue and picked up the clipboard that seemed to be surgically attached to her as of late.

"I think we might want to go for a lighter shade. I like the darker blue, but I wonder if it will seem stifling once it's on the walls. Maybe we should go for more of a sky blue."

Tara appeared to be considering my suggestion. The brighter aqua had been my suggestion in the first place, but now I was afraid it would be too much, especially during the summer months.

"I think you might be right," Tara agreed. "A sky blue or even a light gray. We should look at the paint samples again. The painters are coming back next week to get started, so we need to make a final decision."

I looked around the room we were standing in, which would serve as the coffee bar and bookstore. It was really beginning to look like the space Tara and I had envisioned. A few more weeks and we would be stocking shelves with the inventory we'd ordered.

"Are you going to the mainland tomorrow?" Tara asked.

"Yeah. I planned to attend the adoption clinic in Seattle. We have almost a dozen kittens ready for forever homes."

"Do you think you would have time to stop by the office supply store and have some flyers printed?"

"Yeah, sure. What are the flyers for?"

"The spaghetti dinner at St. Patrick's. The kids are raising funds for a trip at the end of the summer. Sister Mary and I divided up the tasks that needed to be accomplished to make the trip a reality, and fund-raising was one of my chores. I plan to have the dinner on the last Sunday of the month, so I want to get the flyers posted around town as soon as possible."

I looked at Tara, who was looking down at her clipboard. "You and Sister Mary are pretty close."

Tara looked up. "Yeah, I guess so. I've been helping her with the children's program since I was in high school, so we spend a lot of time together."

"Has she ever told you about her past?" I asked.

"Her past?"

"Before she was a nun," I clarified.

Tara frowned. "No. I guess it's never come up. She's been a nun at St. Patrick's since we were in grade school. Why do you ask?"

I hesitated. I wasn't sure I was ready to share my hunch with Tara, or anyone else, just yet.

I shrugged. "I was just curious. With everything that's been going on lately, I've begun to wonder about the past of some of the people we know. Do you want to do a BBQ on the beach tonight?"

"Sounds like fun."

"I'm going to invite Danny and Cody. I'll ask them and then confirm a time with you. I'm thinking we can meet at Sunset Beach at around seven. We can eat and then watch the sun go down. It's been a while since we had a fire on the beach."

"Sounds good. What should I bring?" Tara asked.

"I'll stop by the store and pick something up. You've been carrying the load around here; it's the least I can do."

Tara turned toward the door as two men walked in. They looked like they were there to inspect the property. Because the cannery was such an old building, the council wanted to inspect the construction we'd had done before the paint was applied and the shelving installed. Tara started toward the door to greet the men. It was obvious she would be tied up for a while, so I decided to follow up on the hunch I'd had. It simply wouldn't let go of my imagination no matter how hard I tried to think of other things.

I hoped Sister Mary would not only be in her office but that she'd be alone. The subject I had on my mind wasn't something I wanted to share with anyone else at that point. I realized after I pulled in to the church parking lot that I should have called ahead. But luck was on my side and I found Sister Mary changing over the bulletin boards in the Sunday school room.

"Caitlin, how are you, dear?" Sister Mary asked.

"I'm fine." I fidgeted as I tried to shore up my courage.

"Is there something on your mind?" she asked when I didn't explain the reason for my visit right away.

I took a deep breath and pondered the wisdom of my errand. I remembered what Bella had once told me: you can't unknow what it is you know. Did I really want to know what it was I was there to ask? In the end, my curiosity got the better of me.

"I was wondering if you had a few minutes to chat. Privately," I emphasized.

Sister Mary set down the cutouts she'd been pinning on the board and turned to look at me. "Would you like to go into my office?"

"Yes. That would be best."

I nervously followed the nun down the hall to her office. She indicated that I should have a seat across from her desk. She sat down behind it. I noticed that she'd closed the door. That was good; we wouldn't be interrupted.

"Now, how can I help you?" she asked.

"Destiny Paulson might be pregnant," I blurted out. I knew I'd chickened out, but in the last instant before I spoke, I suddenly doubted I wanted the answer to my real question.

Sister Mary frowned. "Pregnant? Did she tell you as much?"

"No," I admitted. "Trinity mentioned it to me. She overheard her sister talking to a friend. If Trinity is correct and her sister is pregnant, I imagine she must be scared. I got the impression she hasn't told her mother. I considered speaking to her myself, but I know the two of you are close, so I thought that such a delicate topic might be better broached coming from you."

"Yes. I imagine you're right," Sister Mary agreed. "I'll speak to her on Sunday."

I let out a slow breath. It felt good to transfer the responsibility of knowing to someone better equipped to deal with the situation.

"Is that all that's on your mind?" Sister Mary asked.

"Yes." I started to stand up but then changed my mind and sat back down. "No, actually. There's something else."

I took the copy of the newspaper article I'd been carrying around out of my pocket. I slipped it across the desk. Sister Mary glanced at the photo, gasped, and looked up at me.

"Have you told anyone?"

Chapter 10

The evening turned out to be as perfect as I'd hoped. The afternoon had been warm and clear, holding the promise of a spectacular sunset. Danny built a fire in the pit while Cody gathered additional wood and Tara and I set out the picnic I'd thrown together. Max was happily playing with Mr. Parsons's dog, Rambler; Cody had decided to bring him along at the last minute. Given the nature of the conversation I'd planned for later that evening, I'd invited Finn to stop by when he went off duty for the day.

"It really is a perfect night." Tara smiled happily as we sat on the blanket we'd brought along while Cody and Danny tossed a football around on the beach. "Have you heard from Haley?"

"No, but Maggie talked to Delilah when she came by to pick her up. She seemed to think her brother-in-law might welcome a distraction for Haley while he works to get his life back on track. She offered to bring up the subject of Haley staying with Maggie once the funeral is over and the guests have gone home."

"I hope it works out for her. I know Haley was really excited about her summer job working with the cats, and she adores both you and Maggie."

"Yeah," I agreed. "I hope it works out too."

I leaned back on my arms as the last of the warm sun beat down on my tanned legs and face. I loved summer on Madrona Island. Sure, it became crowded at times as visitors from the mainland came over on the ferry for a beach vacation, but the temperatures were usually perfect, the water as clear as you're likely to find anywhere.

"I have the flyer I need copied in my car, so don't leave without it," Tara said.

"Remind me when we leave. How did the inspection go?"

"We're all set to move on to the next phase," she answered. "The painters will get started next week, and I have the flooring company coming in the week after that. The shelving is scheduled to arrive the week following the floor installation, and I hope our inventory will start to show up once the shelves are up. I'm getting more and more excited the closer we get. Aren't you?"

"Um," I replied as the sound of the waves in the distance, coupled with the warm sun on my body and severe sleep deprivation, lulled me toward a relaxed state of consciousness. I let my mind wander to simpler times, when a day at the beach had been nothing more than a day at the beach. Tara and I had been beachaholics when we were in school. From the first day of summer until the last day before the start of the new school year, we'd pack our sunscreen, towels, snacks, and pocket money into backpacks, climb onto our bikes, and head out. Most days we didn't leave the beach until it was time to go home for dinner.

"Max and Rambler seem to be having fun," Tara commented as I felt myself drifting away.

I opened one eye and watched as Cody lobbed a stick he had found into the waves and the dogs raced to fetch it. The tide was low, so the waves, which attracted surfers during high tide, lapped effortlessly onto the sandy shore.

"When are we eating?" Danny wandered over with the football in his hand and sat down next to us. "I'm starving."

"The food is mostly set out. Help yourself," I replied.

"Beer?" Danny asked.

"Blue ice chest."

"Plates?"

"Red striped bag. The rolls are in there too."

"Potato salad?"

"Red ice chest. All the food that isn't already out is either in the bag or the ice chest."

Danny began assembling his plate, and Cody wandered over to make his as well. The four of us ate in silence as I pondered the conversation I planned to initiate once Finn was able to join us. It was going to be a tricky topic to navigate and, not for the first time since my conversation with Sister Mary, I paused to reconsider the wisdom of sharing what I knew.

"You're quiet tonight," Cody commented as the sun began to dip beyond the horizon.

"Just tired," I said.

"I guess it has been a hard few weeks."

I rested my head on Cody's shoulder as the sky turned from yellow to orange and finally red before fading into gray. There was nothing better than a summertime sunset over the ocean.

"I hope Finn gets here soon," I added. "I feel like I'm about to fall asleep."

"Looks like he just pulled into the parking lot," Cody informed me.

I turned to watch as Finn found a spot and then headed our way. The four of us had polished off most of the food, but I'd made sure we'd saved a serving of everything for him. Tara began to assemble his plate as I gathered our trash and Cody tossed another log on the fire. Danny sat strumming his guitar as the sky darkened.

By the time Finn had polished off the last of his meal, the sky had turned black and the stars had begun to arrive in the night sky. The tide was coming in, so the waves grew larger, the gentle lapping onto the shore turning to more of a crashing as the larger waves hit the sandy barrier.

The fire we were gathered around danced in the darkness, providing an eerie setting for an eerie tale.

"I have news," I began as soon as I figured everyone was ready.

"About Orson's murder?" Finn asked as he lounged in one of the beach chairs Cody had set around the fire.

"Indirectly," I answered. "The thing is, what I'm about to tell you absolutely needs to stay between the five of us. If I didn't think this piece of information might be critical in solving Orson's murder, I wouldn't say anything at all."

Everyone except Finn agreed to keep the secret I was about to reveal, and he promised to keep it a secret to the extent that doing so didn't interfere with the murder he was investigating. When everyone was on board I began my tale.

"Cody and I found an old photo taken of a crowd on the ferry while we were looking into the mystery of Jim and Jane Farmington. Standing toward the back of the crowd was a couple who seemed to be standing well away from the others. Cody and I speculated that it could have been Jane and Jim, although we had no way to know for certain. What I did know was that the woman seemed familiar; so familiar, in fact, that my mind wouldn't let go of the idea of placing where I had seen her before."

"I take it you figured it out," Finn responded.

"I did. At three a.m. this morning. Why is it that your mind becomes so much clearer in the middle of the night?"

"So who was it?" Danny asked.

"Sister Mary."

Everyone was silent. Completely silent. I figured they were trying to process the information I'd just spilled.

"The photo of the blond woman on the ferry who we suspected might be Jane Farmington, aka Maryellen Thornton, was really Sister Mary?" Cody clarified.

"The photo was of Sister Mary, Jane Farmington, and Maryellen Thornton. They're all the same person."

"That can't be," Tara insisted.

"I'm afraid it is. Once I realized why the woman on the ferry looked familiar I decided I needed to talk to Sister Mary. As far as I know, no one living knows that Sister Mary is really Maryellen Thornton other than Father Kilian, and now us. Orson knew too."

"But why? How?" Tara asked. "Are you sure?"

I could tell by the shocked expressions on everyone's faces that they were having as hard a time processing this unlikely information as I'd had.

"I went to the church today to speak to Sister Mary," I began. "It took me a while to work up my courage and get to the point, but eventually I showed her the photo that Cody—or I guess I should say Emily—found on the Internet. Sister Mary recognized the photo immediately. As unlikely as it may seem, she confirmed that she is, or maybe I should say was, Maryellen Thornton."

"This doesn't make any sense," Tara said. "Are you certain you heard what you think you heard?"

"I'm sure."

"But why would she be pretending not to be Maryellen?"

"Bear with me while I step you through this," I said to Tara. "Sister Mary told me that she grew up as the only child of a very rich and very rigid couple. While her upbringing was very strict and regimented, she loved her parents and wanted to make them proud. It seemed the only way to do that was to be exceedingly accommodating and obedient, and to keep to herself most of the time. In other words, she learned never to question and always to obey."

I took a deep breath before continuing. "The Thorntons realized the threat of kidnapping was very real, so they sent Maryellen to a private school that had what was at that time a top-of-the-line security system. In addition, the location of the school was kept private, with only those closest to the Thorntons even knowing where she was most of the time. Maryellen lived a very cloistered existence. She wasn't abused, but she wasn't happy either.

"On her tenth birthday," I continued, "Maryellen begged to come home for the week. When her parents agreed, she foolishly—Sister Mary's words—began telling everyone she came into contact with that she was turning ten and going home to celebrate with her family. Sister Mary confided that it was her parents' policy that she never talk about who she was with strangers, but she was so excited that she ignored her parents' dictates. Apparently someone leaked the news to the press, and the next thing she knew, the secret was out."

"Oh God. I can see where this is going." Tara groaned.

"Go on," Danny encouraged.

"On the third night of her visit the family attended the opera. After they returned home Maryellen was sent to bed. She fell asleep quickly but was awakened by a hand being placed over her mouth. She was warned by the intruder not to scream if she didn't want her parents to get hurt. The man picked her up and carried her toward the open window. She panicked and bit the hand that was covering her mouth, and then screamed with all her might. Somehow she managed to wiggle free of his grip and ran toward the door. She opened it to find her parents on the other side. Her kidnapper shot and killed them."

Tara gasped but didn't say anything.

"The kidnapper convinced Maryellen that her parents' death was her fault. If she had kept quiet, like he'd warned her to, he would have ransomed her back and her parents wouldn't have been hurt. He told her he would kill her as well if she didn't do exactly as he instructed. She was terrified, so of course she followed his directions to at T."

"The man who kidnapped her and killed her parents was the same man she was with on the ferry?" Finn asked.

"It was," I verified.

"But why?" Tara asked. "I can see her being terrified as a child, but why didn't she try to escape when she got older?"

"Sister Mary told me that at first she realized that cooperating was the only way she was going to stay alive. And then the years went by, and the man, who called himself Jim Farmington, although she didn't believe that was his real name, took care of her and she came to depend on him. She never stopped fearing him, but she did learn to rely on him. When she was nineteen the couple visited the islands. Sister Mary speculated that this was when the photo of the crowd was taken. Until I showed her it to her, she had no idea of its existence. When she was twenty she became pregnant with Jim's child, although she told me she was never actually married to him."

"He raped her?" Tara asked.

"Sister Mary didn't go into detail and I didn't ask."

"So she became pregnant and they moved to Shelby Island," Cody prodded.

"Yes. Sister Mary said that after she realized she was going to have a child her protective instincts kicked in and she decided it was time to escape. She came up with a plan, but Jim realized what she was up to and stopped her. He threatened to kill both her and the baby if she tried to leave him again, so she didn't. She believes he moved to the island to ensure that she would have nowhere to go should she change her mind about running away. As now, the ferry doesn't stop at Shelby Island. At that time there were very few residents there, so very few neighbors to go to for help."

"I don't get it," Danny interrupted. "If he kidnapped her for ransom why did he keep her all those years?"

"Sister Mary believes he became obsessed with her. She told me that she didn't believe he ever really planned to ransom her to her parents. He just used that as a form of manipulation."

The fire snapped and popped, causing everyone to jump. I looked toward the moonlit sea and tried to calm the emotions I'd been dealing with all day. First Haley's mother had died, and then I had uncovered a secret too horrible to know.

"Okay, so it's ten years after the murder and kidnapping and she's pregnant and living on Shelby Island. What happened?" Finn brought the conversation back around.

I looked directly at him. "Sister Mary said that after her failed escape attempt Jim became even more rigid about controlling her. He kept an almost constant eye on her, and when he wasn't on the property he locked her inside the house. When she went into labor she managed to convince him to call a midwife. She knew that she needed an ally if she was going to protect her child, so she told Jim that things weren't progressing naturally and she would most likely die without help. He finally agreed to fetch the midwife, who was living on Madrona Island at the time. The woman came to Shelby Island on her own boat, which turned out to be nothing short of a miracle. Once he'd arranged for the woman to see to his wife, he went into another room where he got totally drunk. By the time the baby, a girl, was born, Jim was passed out on the floor. Mary said she had a hard labor and delivery and was barely conscious by the time it was over, but she did have the presence of mind to ask the midwife to take the baby and find it a good home. The midwife agreed to take the baby with her when she left and do as she asked. Sister Mary told me that she didn't remember everything they discussed, but she knows she asked the midwife to say the baby had died if anyone asked."

"If Jim was passed out drunk why didn't she just leave with the midwife?" Tara answered.

I watched her face as the shadows cast by the dancing flames revealed her terror as the story unfolded.

"Sister Mary said if she'd left he would have looked for her, and she wanted to make sure the baby was safe. When Jim came to, she told him the baby had died and the midwife had buried it. Mary told me that he'd never wanted the baby, so he didn't seem to care."

"So where does Orson come into all this?" Danny asked.

"As we already know, shortly after Mary delivered her baby, Orson stopped by to congratulate her. She told him the baby had died, but she said he didn't seem convinced. He stopped by several more times, and on one of those occasions Jim saw them talking. Sister Mary told me that Jim was filled with such a jealous rage that he beat her pretty badly. When Orson noticed the bruises the next time he stopped by he called the resident deputy assigned to Madrona Island, who went out to Shelby Island to investigate. Jim swore she had just fallen and hit her face, and she backed him up, so there wasn't much the deputy could do."

"And then?" Tara whispered.

I took a sip of my beer, which had become tepid. My throat felt raw from suppressing the emotions I'd been struggling with all day.

"Sister Mary said that after the deputy visited them, Jim became more and more paranoid, and the beatings came more and more often. One night he beat her until she became unconscious. The next morning she woke up and found that she was lying on the floor in a pool of her own blood. She looked around for Jim, but she didn't see or hear him nearby. The front door was open, which was odd because Jim always locked her in when he left the property. She went into the yard and found Jim's dead body. She told me that she was standing over him when Orson happened by. He believed she had killed her abusive husband, even though she swore she hadn't."

"That must be when he wrote the unpublished article," Cody realized. "I wonder what made Orson change his mind about printing it."

"Sister Mary didn't know. She said he came back the next day. She thought he was there to take her to the sheriff, but he told her he believed her story and was there to help her escape. They used his boat to take Jim's body out to sea. They weighed it down and dumped it overboard. Then he took her to the mainland, where he dropped her off at a church. It was during her time at the church that she decided to leave both Maryellen Thornton and Jane Farmington behind and become Sister Mary. She joined a convent and became a nun. Shortly after that she came back to Madrona Island and has been living at St. Patrick's ever since."

"So she doesn't know who killed Jim?" Finn asked.

"She told me she doesn't. In fact, she said she's gone over it time and time again and can't imagine who would even have known they were living out there on the island."

"And does she know who killed Orson?" Cody asked.

"She claims to have no idea."

"Why did she come back here after all the horrible things that happened in this area?" Tara asked. "Why didn't she move far, far away and start over completely?"

"She wanted to be near her baby," I answered.

"So she knows who adopted her baby?" Tara asked.

"She said she does, but her daughter's identity is a secret she'll take to her grave."

"Wow, that's so . . . wow." Tara gasped. "Does her daughter know the truth?"

"Sister Mary says she doesn't."

"I can't imagine willingly giving up your baby," Tara said sadly. "Although in this situation I guess I can see why she did it."

"I can't imagine giving up all that money," Danny countered. "She's still Maryellen Thornton. All she had to do when she finally got free was return home with her sad tale and she would have been worth hundreds of millions of dollars."

"Sister Mary said she didn't care about the money then, nor does she now. In fact, she considers the money to be a curse. She said she's very content with her life and is depending on us to keep her secret so she can continue being the woman she has molded from the scraps of her past."

"I'll never tell," Tara asserted.

"Yeah, me neither," Danny added.

"Or me," Cody confirmed.

I looked at Finn.

"Are you certain she doesn't know who killed Orson?" Finn asked.

"I'm sure. She's very broken up about his death. He rescued her and gave her a chance at a new life. I honestly believe that if she knew who killed him she would tell someone."

Finn didn't say anything. He didn't promise to keep Sister Mary's secret, but he didn't say he wouldn't either. Finn was a good man. An honorable man. I had to believe that in the end he would do what was right.

Chapter 11

Saturday June 13

By the time I returned to Madrona Island from the mainland, where I had attended the cat adoption clinic, I was exhausted. Getting up at the crack of dawn to make the first ferry off the island in the morning, spending the day talking to prospective adoptive families, and then hurrying back to make the last ferry back to the island made for a long day. Luckily, there was an extra ferry on Friday and Saturday evenings that arrived at the island at nine. If not for that additional late trip I wouldn't be able to make the round trip in one day.

I decided to save myself the effort of cooking dinner and pick up a pizza from Antonio's. I never had had the chance to ask Antonio if Orson had dined in his restaurant the night he'd arrived on the island, so by stopping in to pick up my dinner I hoped to kill two birds with one stone. I called ahead to order a small cheese, my favorite. Maggie had offered to keep both Max and Emily at her house for the day, so I wasn't worried about taking a few extra minutes to pick up dinner before getting home.

"Your pie is all ready," Antonio said when I walked through the door. The restaurant was open until eleven on Saturday nights, and in spite of the late hour there wasn't a table to be had.

I handed him a twenty-dollar bill and he rang up my purchase. "I wanted to ask you if Orson had dinner here last Sunday."

"Yeah, he was in around six. I heard what happened. He was a good man and will be missed."

"Do you remember who he had dinner with?"

Antonio frowned. "I already told all of this to Finn. He warned me that you might come around asking as well. You aren't nosing around where you were told not to, are you?"

"Maybe I am and maybe I'm not. The truth of the matter is, if Orson was here, there would be a lot of people who saw him. If you won't tell me who he had dinner with I'll just keep asking around until I come across someone who saw him."

Antonio laughed. "I see you haven't outgrown your feisty streak."

"So you'll tell me?"

Antonio shrugged. "I don't see how it can hurt. I very much doubt the man Orson dined with is responsible for his death. It was Tripp Brimmer."

I frowned. Tripp Brimmer had been the resident deputy on Madrona Island at the time John Farmington died and Jane Farmington disappeared. I remembered Cody mentioning that Orson had called Tripp about the beatings, and that he'd told him he suspected Jane Farmington was really Maryellen Thornton. I had to wonder if Tripp was in some way involved in what had occurred at the time.

"Thanks for the information and the pizza." I smiled at Antonio. "I guess you're right about Orson's dinner companion not being a suspect. If there's one man on the island who wouldn't hurt a fly it's Tripp."

"Enjoy your pie," Antonio called after me as I headed toward the door.

While I didn't believe Tripp would hurt a fly, I did think he might have information I could use to figure out who'd killed Orson. If he had even been murdered; Finn was still insisting his injuries more closely resembled the effect of a fall rather than an intentional blow to the head. Maybe Finn was right and maybe he wasn't. What I did know was that someone had moved his body, which meant to me that someone had something to hide.

I looked longingly at my pizza. What I really wanted to do was go home, pour myself a glass of wine, and enjoy my cheesy pie. But Tripp lived less than a mile away, and there was a good chance he'd be home at this time of the evening. I could pop by his house, ask a few questions, and then be on my way.

Tripp lived on the water. The house he'd lived in, on a large lot with its own boat dock, had been in his family for three generations. The first thing I noticed when I pulled up was that the boat tied to Tripp's dock mirrored the one Wilbur had described exactly. I hesitated as I tried to make up my mind about following through with my plan to pay the man a visit. I noticed that his car wasn't in the drive, which most likely meant he wasn't home anyway. But there was a light on inside the house, which indicated to me that he would be back shortly if he was away at all.

I thought about what I knew. Tripp was a well-liked and highly respected member of the community. He had served as a deputy for over thirty years and been known as a caring and compassionate man who'd served the law while taking into consideration the individual circumstances behind each case. In other words, he was a kind and fair man. I knew in my gut that Tripp would never kill Orson, but there were a few facts nagging in the back of my brain.

Orson's notes indicated that he'd called Tripp and informed him about his suspicions regarding Jane Farmington. He had responded to his tip but had been unable to act because Jane had insisted she wasn't the missing heiress and her bruises were the result of a fall. I doubted Tripp had believed Jane Farmington, even if he didn't have a basis on which to act.

I also knew that Tripp, probably more than anyone on the island other than Finn, would have the ability to put a notification order on county records, especially those records dating back to the days when he was the deputy on Madrona Island. Cody and I suspected that if Orson had been murdered because of what he knew, Finn's snooping around in the old files could have been what had alerted the killer that someone had talked.

If Tripp had had dinner with Orson on Sunday that gave him opportunity, but I still didn't see him having a clear motive to kill the man. I had all but decided to head home and call Finn when Tripp pulled into his drive. He noticed my car and headed toward me.

"Caitlin Hart. What are you doing sitting in front of my house?"

"I just picked up a pizza at Antonio's." I tried to keep my sudden nervousness from my voice.

"And you wanted to share it?"

"Uh, yeah, sure. I hope you like cheese."

"I love cheese. Come on in and I'll get us something to drink."

I reluctantly left the safety of my car to follow Tripp inside. I couldn't help but glance at the boat tied to his dock as we neared the house. I couldn't tell if it had a red spotlight, but the shape definitely matched the description Wilbur had given me.

"Been fishing lately?" I asked.

"Unfortunately, my motor is fried. I've been waiting almost three weeks for a replacement. Figures the old girl would give out at the beginning of the season."

If Tripp was telling the truth it couldn't have been him Wilbur had seen. But if he was lying…

"That's too bad. I hope you get her up and running soon."

I took a seat at Tripp's kitchen table while he poured us each an iced tea. He set a glass in front of me along with a bowl of sugar. "So what's on your mind?" he asked.

"What makes you think there's anything on my mind?" I asked.

"'Cause you've known me your whole life and this is the first time you've come for a visit."

"Yeah, I guess you have a point." I took a sip of my tea as a means of stalling.

"How about I help us get started?" Tripp smiled. "You went to Antonio's to get a pizza, and while you were there Antonio happened to mention that I had dinner with Orson on the evening he died. In spite of the fact that Finn has asked you to stay out of it, your natural inclination is to be right in the middle of things. When you heard I'd dined with Orson you realized I could be a suspect, so you hightailed it over here without once stopping to think that if I was guilty of killing Orson, coming to my home alone would be a really, really stupid thing to do."

"Yeah, something like that," I agreed.

"I didn't kill Orson."

"Honestly, I really didn't think you had, but there are some interesting facts that point to you as the killer."

"Such as?" Tripp asked.

"For one thing, I suspect Orson's death could be due to an old mystery Cody West and I have been looking into. It pertains to a couple, Jim and Jane Farmington, who lived on Shelby Island twenty-six years ago. I know you responded to a tip from Orson that Jane Farmington might be Maryellen Thornton, the missing heiress, and that Jane was being abused. I know you were unable to arrest Jim because Jane refused to verify Orson's accusations. I also know that when Jim Farmington was found dead Orson helped Jane get rid of the body and escape. I have to assume something happened to cause him to realize she hadn't killed her husband as he'd originally believed."

I wasn't sure giving Tripp all this information was a wise idea, but Orson was dead, so he couldn't be prosecuted for his part in the cover-up, and I doubted Tripp knew what had become of Jane.

"Orson tell you all that?"

"Yes," I lied. It was actually Sister Mary who had told me, but that wasn't something I was about to share with Tripp.

"I did respond to Orson's tip and he was correct that there was nothing I could do to help Jane if she was unwilling to help herself. I continued to visit the island to monitor the situation. The man was a monster. I was afraid he was going to kill her." Tripp looked me in the eye. "In fact, he almost did. On the night he died he beat Jane until she was unconscious."

"You were at the island the night Jim Farmington died?" I asked.

"Like I said, after that first time I started stopping by to check on things from a distance. Jane was a pretty little thing with a quick mind and a lot of potential, but she was about as timid as anyone I'd ever met."

"Did you talk to her on other visits?"

"A time or two," Tripp confirmed.

"So you showed up while Jim was beating Jane. What did you do?"

Tripp looked away. He didn't say anything, but I could see he knew something.

"You killed him," I realized. It was the only thing that made any sense. Orson had found the body and realized Jane had been beaten, so he decided she must have killed her husband in self-defense. He'd notified Tripp, who at that point confided in Orson that he'd been out to the property to check on her and had witnessed at least the end of the beating. He'd killed the man and then confided in Orson, who helped to cover it up.

"I didn't mean to," Tripp admitted. "I went out there to check on things and saw John kicking Jane. She was already on the ground, and as far as I could tell already unconscious. I broke in through the front door and Jim came at me with a butcher knife. I was off duty, so my gun was in my car, not on my person. Jim and I struggled. Eventually, we wound up outside. Jim ended up with the knife in his chest and died before I could do anything to help him. I'm not proud of it, but I panicked and took off. I didn't even go back to see if Jane was still alive."

"Wow."

"Wow is right. I regret everything that happened that night. I handled the entire thing badly. When I confessed to Orson what had occurred he convinced me that no good would come from confessing to Jim's murder. No one even knew he was dead. Heck, no one even knew he was on the island. Orson told me that he'd take care of things, and he did. He assured me Jane was safe and had found a better life, so I pushed the whole thing to the back of my mind." Tripp looked me directly in the eye. "I would *never* hurt Orson. He took a chance and saved me. I don't know who killed him, but I'm as anxious as you to find out."

I really didn't know what to say. Orson had been right; no good would have come from prosecuting Tripp for his part in Jim Farmington's death. Orson felt it was best to cover it up, and I found I had to agree.

"I won't tell anyone," I whispered.

"I appreciate that. Looking back, I'm not sure whether Orson and I did the right thing. Jim Farmington was a monster who deserved to die, but not Orson. If he was killed because of the events of that night I don't know how I'll ever live with it."

"Is that why you and Orson met for dinner?" I asked. "So he could fill you in on the fact that Cody and I were snooping around?"

"The subject came up, but mostly he just wanted to say good-bye. I think he was happy to be moving to the East Coast to be near his family, but I don't think he realized how hard it would be to say good-bye to the island he'd lived on his entire life."

"Did he mention anyone else he planned to visit?"

"Not specifically. I know he planned to meet with Cody on Monday, and he mentioned there were a few others he wanted to say good-bye to, but he didn't elaborate."

"Based on the fact that his mail was still on the floor of the entry of his house, it appears he never made it home. Do you know where he went after he left Antonio's?"

"I believe he was headed to the newspaper office. He said earlier in our conversation that he had a notebook and an unpublished edition of the *Madrona Island News* that he hoped to remove from the premises before Cody found them. I take it based on this conversation that he was too late?"

I nodded. "Cody found the journal and the newspaper before Orson arrived on the island. He called to speak to him about it, but his son told him Orson was already on his way west. So you think he was headed to the newspaper office when he left the restaurant?"

"I believe so, although he didn't actually say that. We finished eating around seven thirty, we hugged and promised to keep in touch, and then he drove off toward Pelican Bay and I came home."

"What kind of car was he driving?" I asked.

"It was a rental. A dark blue Ford Focus."

I realized for the first time that the whereabouts of the car Orson had been driving could give us a clue as to what had happened to him. I hadn't thought to look for a car, and Cody hadn't mentioned it either. Perhaps Finn had already looked into it.

"Do you remember anything specific about the car? License number? Identification sticker?"

Tripp shook his head. "I didn't know what was going to happen, so I didn't pay that much attention. I do remember that the interior was a really light color. Not white, but close to it. The reason I know that is because I remember thinking it was a ridiculous interior color for a rental car. It must be impossible to keep clean."

"Okay, thanks. Let me know if you think of anything else."

Now all I had to do was drive around the island and look for a dark blue Focus with a light color interior. Of course it was dark, and I wasn't likely to find the car at night, so I drove down the street where the newspaper office was located for good measure and then headed home.

Chapter 12

By the time I finally made it home Maggie had already gone up to bed, so she'd returned Max and Emily to my cabin. It was a warm evening, so I poured myself a glass of wine, pulled on a heavy sweatshirt, and sat down on one of the chairs on the deck. Emily curled up in my lap while Max ran around on the beach just to the side of the deck. I was contemplating whether to call Cody when my phone rang.

"I was just thinking about you," I answered.

"Sounds promising," Cody teased.

"In your dreams." I laughed. "What's up?"

"I came by your cabin earlier, but you weren't there yet. I knew you planned to return on the last ferry so when you weren't home I was concerned you'd missed it."

"I decided to stop by to pick up a pizza. I happened to ask Antonio about Orson's dinner companion, who turned out to be Tripp."

"So you went to talk to Tripp," Cody concluded.

"Yup."

"And?"

I hesitated. "It's kind of a long and involved story. It might be better to talk about it in person."

"Mr. Parsons is in bed," Cody said. "It'd only take me five minutes to walk down the beach. I was going to take Rambler out anyway."

"Okay. I'm sitting on the deck. I'll see you in a few."

After I hung up I thought about whether I should tell Cody everything I'd learned from Tripp. On one hand, I'd promised him I wouldn't tell. On the other, I felt like Cody and I had developed a relationship where we shared everything. It didn't seem right to keep such an important secret, especially because it was directly related to the mystery we'd been working on. The fact that I felt this way about Cody when he'd only been back in my life for a few weeks was a freak-out for another day. I'd been hurt by Cody once, and even if it had been pretty much 100 percent my own fault, I still felt the need to take things slowly as we reestablished our relationship.

I looked out onto the smooth surface of the ocean. The waves were calmly lapping onto the shore this evening, barely creating a ripple on the moonlit surface. It was the perfect night for romance, but the only thing on my mind—at least I told myself it was the only thing on my mind—was murder. Specifically, who had murdered Orson Cobalter.

Emily hopped down from my lap and wandered over to the edge of the deck. I'd never seen her jump from the deck down onto the sand. I don't think she knew quite what to make of what she'd done. Max trotted over to greet her, and the two animals stood nose to nose as they said their hellos.

Emily looked up as Rambler came running down the beach with Cody behind him. She hunched her back in a show of irritation before running back to the deck to jump into my lap. I scratched her behind the ears as Cody reached me and Max and Rambler took off, chasing each other around in circles.

"Beautiful night," Cody commented as he sat down next to me. His feet were bare, but he had on worn and faded jeans and a light blue hoodie.

"It really is. I've just been sitting here looking at the reflection of the moon on the water. I really should go to bed, but I can't quite seem to shut down my mind. At least not yet."

"Long day?" Cody asked.

"The longest."

"Successful?"

"Placed all the kittens into what appear to be really good homes," I confirmed.

"That's good."

Cody tossed a stick that was lying near his feet into the surf for the dogs to fetch. "So you had a chat with Tripp?"

"I did," I said. I sat quietly for a minute while I gathered my thoughts. "Here's the thing," I began. "I'm going to share with you some interesting and some might even say shocking news, but before I do, you have to promise not to tell anyone. Not even Danny. Not even Finn."

"Okay," Cody agreed slowly. I could tell he was hesitant to promise to keep a secret he hadn't yet heard, but I was sure he was even more curious.

I shared the content of my conversation with Tripp, including the part where he admitted to being responsible for Jim Farmington's death and then working with Orson to cover the whole thing up.

Cody whistled.

"I can't imagine having to live with that your whole life. Or at least most of your life. He must have already been in his forties when the incident occurred."

"Did you get the impression he knows who Sister Mary is?"

"No," I answered. "He didn't bring it up, but I didn't get the feeling he ever knew what happened to Jane Farmington. He just said Orson assured him that she was safe and had created a new life. He lives on the island, but he attends the community church, not St. Patrick's, so he may not have had any reason to ever meet her."

"And when you spoke to her did you get the impression that Sister Mary knows who killed Jim and why?"

"She told me she didn't know. I have no reason not to believe her."

"And Finn?"

"Doesn't know," I confirmed. "We can't tell him. He'd be obligated to act on the information, and I don't see that it would serve any purpose at this point. Tripp isn't a violent or dangerous man. He became entangled in a complicated situation twenty-six years ago that he may have handled badly, but I can't see any reason to mess up his life now. No one other than Sister Mary, Orson, and Tripp even knew Jim Farmington had died."

Cody sighed. "I don't disagree with you. Tripp is a good man. It sounds like the whole thing was just a tragic accident. I don't believe Tripp is a dangerous man, nor do I think he should be punished now for making what some might consider to be a bad choice by not alerting the authorities to Jim Farmington's death."

"He seemed haunted by his decision," I confirmed.

"We've uncovered a lot of information and have been privy to some pretty spectacular secrets over the past week, but we really aren't any closer to solving Orson's murder than we were when we started."

"That's true. Although Tripp did say he thought Orson was heading over to the newspaper office to retrieve his notebook and the uncirculated newspaper before you discovered it. That means he wasn't aware you'd already found it. If he didn't know that he wouldn't have necessarily been on the island to warn anyone. Maybe his death really doesn't have anything to do with the old mystery."

"Maybe," Cody agreed. "But if not that, then what? Another secret about another article we haven't stumbled across?"

"Maybe," I said. "You've spent a lot of time at the paper the past couple of weeks. Have you noticed that anything was disturbed? Other files or newspapers we hadn't been looking through?"

"No." Cody shook his head. "Not really. I wasn't looking for anything to be disturbed, and there was definitely nothing obvious. Which makes it seem like Orson never made it to the newspaper office. If he had I would guess he would have moved at least some things around looking for the journal and the old newspaper."

"Unless he realized right off that the journal and newspaper were gone and left," I suggested.

"Yeah, that makes sense."

"I wish I knew where he was heading next. He obviously didn't go home."

"Tripp didn't have any ideas?" Cody asked.

"No, he just said Orson indicted he had a couple more people to say good-bye to and planned to stop by the newspaper office. He didn't seem to know who the *couple more people* were, though."

"Did you ever have a chance to ask Danny about the boat Wilbur saw the night Orson was killed?"

"Yeah. He said there were a lot of boats that fit the description. He did think the red spotlight could be unique, but he didn't know of a boat that had one offhand. He's pretty familiar with all the boats that dock in Pelican Bay, so he figures this one either docks in Harthaven Harbor or it could have come in from out of the area. Tripp has a boat that matches the description, but he said it's out of service, and after all that he shared I have no reason to believe he'd lie about that."

Emily got up from my lap and headed toward the door leading into the cabin. I figured she wanted food or water, both of which I'd filled before coming out, so I let her inside. I returned to my chair, and Cody and I sat in silence as we engaged in our own thoughts. A few minutes later Emily was scratching at the door to get out.

"Silly cat," I complained as I got up for the second time.

Emily greeted me at the door with a sheet of paper in her mouth. I took it from her and looked at it. It was the note that had been left on my windshield, telling me to mind my own business. In any other circumstance I'd have ignored that note, but I was beginning to learn that the cats that were coming into my life were there for a purpose. I handed the note to Cody, then gathered Emily into my arms and sat down.

"What is this?" he asked.

I explained about the scratch on my car, as well as the note that had been left the previous Sunday.

"Any idea who left it?" Cody asked.

"Not a clue."

Cody frowned. "This note seems to insinuate that someone knew you were nosing around into the old mystery, but as of Sunday morning no one other than you and I knew anything at all about it. We hadn't even talked about it to Finn, Tara, and Danny yet."

"That's true, but what else could it be about?"

Cody stared at the note. "I'm not sure, but I don't like it at all. Do you remember anything odd that happened that morning?"

"Trinity Paulson was sick. I went into the girls' bathroom to see how she was, and during the course of our conversation she told me Destiny might be pregnant. She begged me not to tell anyone, but I did say I was going to talk to Destiny. I suppose Trinity might have told Destiny before Tara took them home. I guess it's possible the note could be from her."

"An intentional scratch does sound more like a teen thing," Cody agreed. "Anything else?"

"After I found the note I went into the bathroom to change for the softball game and I overheard two men talking. They were passing by the door in the hallway so I only heard a few sentences of their conversation. The men seemed concerned about someone's interference in something, and the first man was assuring the second one that he'd take care of it. That's all I heard."

"Did you recognize either voice?" Cody asked.

"No. And by the time I peeked out the door they were turning the corner. I did see one man for just a second from the back. He was tall with gray hair."

"And you said this occurred after you found the note?"

"Yes."

Cody wrinkled his brow. "Chances are these men didn't leave the note. My vote is for Destiny for that. We'll ask her tomorrow. The conversation you overheard concerns me, though, especially considering what happened to Orson that night. I wish we had more to go on."

"I believe I saw their vehicles," I offered. "When I went out to my car the first time I remember noticing there were only three vehicles left in the parking lot. When I came back from changing my car was the only one left."

"And the others?" Cody asked.

I closed my eyes and tried to remember. "One was a truck. An older model with a lift kit. I think it was black. The other was a four-door sedan. I don't remember what kind, but it was white."

"Did you see a license plate?" Cody asked.

"No. To be honest, I was more focused on the scratch on my car than I was on either of the other vehicles in the parking lot."

"I want you to look around the parking lot tomorrow during church. See if you recognize either vehicle. If you do just write down the license number. Don't do anything else."

I frowned.

"Promise me."

"Okay, I promise. By the way, as long as we're discussing cars, Tripp told me Orson was driving a rental when they met for dinner. A dark blue Ford Focus with a light interior. This isn't a very big island; I don't think it would be impossible to find it. If we can find the car we might be able to figure out what Orson was doing or who he was meeting with just before he died."

Cody furrowed his brow. "I've seen a car that meets that description. It's parked on the side street near the church. I noticed it when we were there on Wednesday for choir practice."

"I wonder what Orson was doing at the church."

"You said Orson knew Sister Mary's secret. I imagine they stayed friends. Maybe he was there to say good-bye to her."

"She didn't tell me he'd stopped by when I spoke to her," I informed him.

"Maybe she didn't think it was relevant to your conversation."

"I kind of doubt that. We were talking about finding Orson's killer. I'm sure if she had seen him since his return to the island she would have mentioned it."

"Perhaps. I guess it wouldn't hurt to ask her tomorrow. If Orson wasn't at the church to visit with her, maybe he was there to see Father Kilian. We should ask him as well."

I frowned. "You realize the last person to visit with Orson is most likely the one who killed him."

Cody shrugged. "Not necessarily. All we can do is follow the clues to see where they lead."

I remembered Tansy's warning: *There are many things you're destined to find and many things you're destined to know. Just remember, with knowing comes a burden that, at times, is best carried alone.* If the knowing had anything to do with the two remaining staff at the church, I was pretty sure I *didn't* want to know.

Chapter 13

Sunday, June 14

One of these days I'm going to wake up and *not* be nervous about what the day might bring. Unfortunately, today was not that day. Cody and I not only planned to speak to both Sister Mary and Father Kilian about possible visits from Orson but we also planned to track down the men I'd heard outside the bathroom door at the church. To make matters worse, I knew Sister Mary was going to speak to Destiny about her possible pregnancy, and I was certain the girl would know I was the one who'd ratted her out. If this day didn't end in tears all around it was going to be a flat-out miracle.

I rolled out of bed and began my morning routine. I let Max out the side door, tossed a match on the fire, and started a pot of coffee. I filled Emily's food and water dishes, and once the coffee was ready I filled my favorite Garfield mug and wandered over to the sofa. I'd barely sat down when Max came to the door, announcing his desire to come back in. I set the coffee aside and went to the door. The minute I opened the door for Max, Emily squeezed through and darted out onto the deck.

"Emily, what's up?" I asked tiredly. She'd never pushed her way through the door in quite that manner before. She walked over to the hat Max had found in the ocean the other day and began to meow.

"I forgot to take that old thing to the trash," I replied. "It's nothing important, just some old thing Max found. Now let's go inside. It's cold."

The kitten sat on the hat and refused to move. I couldn't imagine what had gotten into the feline. The hat had been sitting on the deck for several days and she hadn't paid a bit of attention to it until now. I was about to pick her up and forcefully bring her into the house when it occurred to me that she might be trying to tell me something. I picked up the hat and looked at it more closely. It was a baseball-style cap with the name of a local whale-watching charter stitched on the outside. Orcas and More was a relatively new business. If I remembered correctly, Danny had first mentioned the company's arrival in the area the previous summer. At first he'd been concerned about the increase in competition, but the last time I'd talked to him about the new rival, he reported that they didn't seem to be actively providing charters, although he had seen the boat trolling around from time to time. He told me that in spite of the fact that the boat seemed to be out on the water, he'd never seen it carrying any passengers. He wondered why they'd bothered to set up shop on the island if they weren't going to provide tours.

Could they be doing something illegal? Maybe something like smuggling stolen items or transporting drugs? The border between the United States and Canada was barely a stone's throw away, and to the west of that was international water. It occurred to me that it might be interesting to take a closer look at their activities, but the last thing I had time to do was ponder the motivation of one of Danny's competitors.

I filed the bit of information concerning the charter company in the back of my mind and then promptly forgot about it. Maybe once we'd found Orson's killer I'd mention the odd behavior of the charter boat to Cody.

I picked up the kitten and headed inside to have breakfast and get ready for church.

Several hours later I was walking back and forth along the rows of cars parked in the parking lot at St. Patrick's, looking for the black truck or white sedan I'd seen the previous Sunday. For all I knew, neither of the two men I'd overheard were even attending Mass today. Tara was helping Cody get the children's choir ready to go on while Sister Mary chatted with Destiny. Cody and I had shown up early in order to ask Sister Mary and Father Kilian if they'd spoken to

Orson, but both responded that they hadn't seen him, which left me to wonder what his rental car was doing parked on the street across from the church. There were a lot of things about this case that were puzzling. In fact, when I really thought about it, *everything* about this case was puzzling.

I was about to give up and go inside when I noticed the black truck I'd seen the week before three rows over. I looked around, but Mass was just about to begin, so there were few stragglers still in the parking lot. I knew Cody wanted me to get the license plate number and then leave the truck alone, but I figured it couldn't hurt to take a peek inside. I jogged across the lot and looked in through the passenger side window. The first thing I noticed was an Orcas and More hat on the backseat. I felt a tingling that started at the base of my spine and work its way up to my neck. There was no way this could be a simple coincidence.

I walked around to the bed of the truck and looked over the side. It was covered by a blue waterproof tarp. It was tied down, but I lifted one corner and peeked inside. It was dark under the tarp, but I could see there was a lot of stuff stored in the truck. It looked like the sort of equipment you would use in a dredging operation.

I looked around the deserted parking lot again. I could hear the choir singing the first of the three opening songs we'd prepared. The only way I was going to get a better look at the contents of the truck bed was to loosen the ropes, but I doubted I could get them tightened back the way they'd been. I was small, and the opening I'd created was small too. Perhaps I could just squeeze inside, take a look around, and squeeze back out. What could it hurt?

I slid inside the opening on my stomach and then scooted around so I could get a look at the entire contents of the truck bed. As I suspected, there appeared to be a lot of equipment that would be used to dredge the bottom of a sandy surface, along with scuba tanks, regulators, and other diving gear. The equipment in the truck had to be worth thousands of dollars. I couldn't imagine why the owner of the truck would leave it out in the open for anyone to steal.

I was about to climb back out of the truck when I heard voices. My heart began to pound as I listened.

"I told you that I was going to pick you up in the parking lot," a man with a deep voice said.

"I know, but my wife asked me to drop the kids off for choir," a second man replied. Now that he'd made a reference to the choir, I realized the second man was Pete Valdez. Pete was the father of two of our choir members. I didn't really know him, nor did I know what he did for a living. "What was I going to do? I couldn't very well tell them to find their own way inside."

"I have a lot of expensive equipment under that tarp. The last thing I wanted to do was leave it unattended while I went to look for you."

Please don't look. Please don't look.

I lay as quietly as I could, praying the men couldn't hear my heartbeat, which was pounding in my ears.

"It was only a few minutes. It looks like everything is fine," Pete answered. "I have to be back to get the kids in two hours, so we'd better get going."

I listened as the men climbed into the truck. I let out a silent groan when the engine was ignited. This wasn't going to turn out well.

At least I had my phone with me. I texted both Finn and Cody to explain my predicament. Cody was busy with the kids and most likely wouldn't have a chance to check his phone until after the opening set, but maybe Finn? All I could do was pray that one of them would come find me before the men in the cab thought to look under the tarp.

I needed to figure out where we were going. I didn't dare risk poking my head out to take a look, so I concentrated on the left and right turns we took. It felt like we were heading toward Harthaven Harbor. When I heard the sound of the flocks of seagulls that hung out at the harbor, waiting for the scraps the local fishermen threw overboard, I knew I had most likely guessed correctly.

When the truck stopped I began to panic. My instinct was to climb out and try to run, but the men would easily be able to grab me before I untangled myself from the tarp.

I heard the men open the doors to the passenger section of the truck and step outside.

"I thought you said she'd be here," Pete commented.

"She'll be here," the man with the deeper voice answered.

"I have a bad feeling," Pete said. "I don't know why I let you talk me into this. We weren't doing that bad. It would have been a lot safer to stick with selling the stuff we found on the wreck."

"We've been working that wreck for a year. We've barely covered our costs," the man reminded Pete. "The information we have is going to make us a hundred times what we'd ever pull off that boat. It's a no-brainer. We have a good plan. We just need to stick to it."

"I'm not sure this is quite the no-brainer you keep telling me it is. Things don't seem to be working out the way we talked about," Pete argued.

"What things?"

"Killing the old man, for one thing."

"That was unfortunate," the man with the deep voice agreed. "The odds were a million to one that he would show up during the break-in. I could never have predicted that."

"I feel like the old guy's death changes things."

"It doesn't change anything. What happened was unfortunate, but there's no way anyone is going to link him back to us. We just need to offer the proof and collect the ransom."

Ransom?

"What if you're wrong?" Pete asked.

"I'm not wrong. Here she comes."

I held my breath and waited. Really, that was all I could do. I hoped and prayed that the men would have no reason to look under the tarp. It didn't sound like they were going dredging, so maybe I'd get out of this in one piece. I realized I really should text Cody and Finn again to let them know I was at the marina. That way at least they'd know where to find my beaten and bloody body should it come to that.

"You have the money?" the man with the deep voice asked whoever walked up.

"You have the proof?" a woman asked.

I could hear the rustle of papers being passed around.

"How do I know this is real?" the woman asked.

"I brought photos as well as the hairbrush we stole. Have the DNA tested for yourself if you don't believe me."

"And she doesn't know anything about this?" she asked.

"Not a thing. You give us the money and we'll be on our way, never to speak about this again."

I couldn't help but try to work out what was going on while I hid. If nothing else, it gave me something to think about other than being discovered. It sounded like Pete and his friend had been in the middle of a heist of some type when Orson came along. Based on the fact that we'd found Orson's car across from the church, it seemed reasonable to assume that the men were stealing something from one of the buildings on the property belonging to St. Patrick's. The men must have hit Orson over the head and then transported him to the place I'd found him.

Poor Orson.

"How do I know this isn't a double cross?" I heard the woman say.

"Why would we do that?" the man who wasn't Pete asked.

"Money makes people do crazy things."

"We aren't going to double-cross you. We have a piece of information to sell, and once we've done that you'll never see or hear from us again."

"I could just kill you," the woman stated.

I gasped. I put my hand over my mouth, hoping no one had heard me.

"We thought of that," the man with the deep voice offered. "We have a third partner. If anything happens to us, there's a file that will be sent to every major newspaper in the country, revealing that Maryellen Thornton is alive and well and her family has known about it all along but never revealed the fact because they wanted to keep her inheritance to themselves. The packet includes photos of Sister Mary, as well as the DNA results from the evidence we gathered."

No one spoke for a minute.

"Look," Pete spoke to the woman for the first time, "two million dollars is a lot of money to us. Enough to keep us quiet. It's a drop in the bucket to you. I doubt you'll miss it. It seems your best bet is to trust that we'll do as we say. We have families. Kids. We aren't going to double-cross you."

"And this third person?"

"The third person I mentioned is the one who knew Sister Mary was Maryellen in the first place. This person has kept the secret all these years. This person isn't going to start blabbing now."

A person who knew about it all these years? Orson knew, but he was dead. Father Kilian knew, but he would never be working with these guys. Tripp Brimmer? Damn. I should have known the guy was doing the old double-talk routine with me.

"Okay. The bulk of the money will be transferred to the bank account you provided after we've confirmed your test results. The cash deposit we talked about is in the bag."

"Been nice doing business with you," the man with the deep voice said.

I listened as the woman walked away.

"Guess we should be going," Pete commented.

"I want to put this stuff in the boat first," the second man said. "It'll just take a minute."

I felt myself begin to hyperventilate as the rope on one corner of the tarp was loosened. There was no way they weren't going to see me. I could try to run, but I'd have to untangle myself and hop up and over the side of the truck bed. I was never going to make it. I tried to calm my churning stomach as the men began to loosen the second corner.

I looked around for a weapon, but there was nothing small enough for me to pick up and swing. I felt the cool air as a corner of the tarp was lifted. I prayed harder than I'd ever prayed in my life that someone, anyone, would come along and rescue me.

"Morning, Pete; Nolte."

I let out the breath I'd been holding as whoever was about to pull back the tarp laid it down again.

Nolte? I tried to remember if I knew anyone named with that name, but I was coming up blank. The two men were obviously partners in some sort of salvage operation. I remembered the hat. Maybe they were the men who'd moved to the island to operate Orcas and More but ended up salvaging a wreck instead.

"Deputy Finnegan," one of the men responded. "Can we help you with something?"

"I hope so," Finn replied.

I crawled out from under the tarp. "These are the men who killed Orson," I shouted as soon as I'd freed myself.

Both men looked shocked as I jumped out of the truck.

"You don't say." Finn smiled as he pulled his gun on them.

Chapter 14

Friday July 3

It had been an eventful two and a half weeks since Finn saved me at the marina. Every time I think life is going to level out and I can shift into cruise control for a while, something new comes along and demands my attention.

First Pete and Nolte, who did turn out to be the owners of Orcas and More, had been arrested for killing Orson, and I had spent the better part of the day telling and retelling Finn everything I had overheard. At first the men weren't giving up the third accomplice, but after Finn worked on them for a while they'd admitted that the third partner had not been Tripp, as I'd suspected, but the midwife who had delivered Maryellen's baby. It seemed Maryellen had confessed everything to the midwife during her long hours of labor. She'd been in a state of delirium toward the end of a very long, difficult labor and delivery and hadn't remembered that. The midwife had sat on the knowledge all these years until her nephew, Pete, had mentioned to her that he and Nolte might need to give up on the salvage of the ship they had found due to a lack of money to continue with the project.

In other news, Haley had come back to Madrona Island with plans to stay until school started after Labor Day. It was decided that she would stay with Maggie because Delilah was even more behind in her painting after having taken two weeks off to go home to bury her sister. Maggie was in seventh heaven having Haley to dote on twenty-four hours a day, and Haley seemed just as thrilled with the arrangement. The best part of all from the girl's perspective was that her dad had promised to let her bring home one of the cats from the sanctuary, now that her mother's illness was no longer an issue. In spite of my own fondness for this particular feline, it seemed that Haley and Emily had bonded in a way I knew Emily and I never would, so I'd agreed to let her go. Besides, it looked as if Emily had finished giving the help she'd shown up on my doorstep to provide.

Looking back, I couldn't have solved the case without Emily. She'd been the one to pounce on the computer in just the right way to cause it to open to the page with the photo of Jim and Jane Farmington on the ferry. If not for that photo, Cody and I might never have discovered Orson's secret. And although Max had found the Orcas and More hat in the surf, it had been Emily who had brought it to my attention. If not for the hat on the backseat of the truck I might never have decided to look under the tarp, climb inside, and take the fateful journey to the marina. And if I hadn't overheard the conversation between Maryellen Thornton's greedy relative and Pete and Nolte, we might never have found out who'd killed Orson.

Besides, when I looked at Emily and Haley together I knew in my heart that they were meant for each other. Emily had obviously been separated from her mom at a much too young age, as had Haley. If you ask me, they've found comfort in each other. It was rare to find the two lost souls apart from each other for any length of time.

As for the condominium project that had had everyone up in arms, it had been permanently placed on the back burner until all the attorneys for everyone involved had a chance to sort things out. The way it looks to me, the project is dead. Banjo doesn't want to sell, the council doesn't want to take legal action to force him, and Bill Powell has made his position regarding the necessity of water access more than clear. I just hope that once the dust settles, the peace and camaraderie that the island's residents have always enjoyed will return without too much long-term damage.

The remodel of the old cannery into Coffee Cat Books is right on schedule. The paint has been applied and the flooring has been installed. The carpenters are just finishing up with the installation of the coffee counter and the shelving to display the inventory. The grand opening is scheduled for August 1, and I have to admit I'm as excited for the big day as anyone in town. Although we aren't yet open for business, Tara and I have decided to announce to the island our grand opening plans by entering a float in the annual Fourth of July parade. Haley and I have been working almost nonstop on a float featuring a giant cat sitting in a chair reading. Next to the cat is a round side table and on the table is a replica of the pink Coffee Cat Books cups we plan to feature.

There's just one dark spot on my otherwise awesome life. Cody plans to leave the island on the Monday following the holiday to wrap things up with the Navy and to pack up his stuff for his permanent move to the island. I know he'll be back, so I'm surprised that I'm dreading his time away as much as I am. At times I'm concerned about how easily I've fallen back in love with the man I vowed to avoid until my dying day. I'm not certain how he feels about me, and this time around I am *not* going to make the first move.

As they do every year on July 3, the business owners who have planned to enter floats in the parade, which will be held after the pancake breakfast the following day, are sequestered in someone's garage, putting the final touches on their projects. Maggie and Marley decided to help Tara and me with our float rather than entering their own this year, so there was a large crowd gathered at Maggie's estate for float assembly and BBQ.

"The float is absolutely adorable," Sister Mary commented as I worked to secure the crepe paper we used to fill in the mug.

"Thank you. We've been working really hard on it," I said.

"I'm so proud of both of you girls," Sister Mary commented. "You set a goal, you worked hard, and you accomplished what you set out to do. There aren't a lot of people who could have turned that old cannery into a wonderful, inviting space the way you and Tara have."

"It was really Tara who worked the miracle," I told her. "I helped, but it was her brain child. She's really something."

"Yes." Sister Mary turned her head to look at Tara. "She is."

Sister Mary smiled as Tara laughed at something Maggie had just said. My heart skipped a beat at the likeness of both their smiles and their profiles. Suddenly I knew.

I looked across the lawn at Tansy, who winked at me as I remembered her words.

There are many things you're destined to find and many things you're destined to know. Just remember, with knowing comes a burden that, at times, is best carried alone.

Kathi Daley lives with her husband, kids, grandkids, and Bernese mountain dogs in beautiful Lake Tahoe. When she isn't writing, she likes to read (preferably at the beach or by the fire), cook (preferably something with chocolate or cheese), and garden (planting and planning, not weeding). She also enjoys spending time on the water when she's not hiking, biking, or snowshoeing the miles of desolate trails surrounding her home.

Made in the USA
Las Vegas, NV
06 December 2023

82202716R00115